BEDTIME EYES

also by amy yamada

Trash

BEDTIME
EYES

*   *   *

amy yamada

translated by yumi gunji
and marc jardine

ST. MARTIN'S PRESS ⚜ NEW YORK

This book is being published within the Japanese Literature Publishing Program, managed by the Japan Association for Cultural Exchange on behalf of the Agency for Cultural Affairs of Japan.

www.stmartins.com

Library of Congress Cataloging-in-Publication Data

Yamada, Amy, 1959–
    [Beddo taimu aizu. English]
    Bedtime eyes / by Amy Yamada; translated by Yumi Gunji and Marc Jardine.
      p.   cm.
    ISBN 0-312-35226-3
    EAN 978-0-312-35226-4
    I. Gunji, Yumi.   II. Jardine, Marc.
    PL865.A489B43   2006
    895.6"35—dc22
                                                2005052041

First Edition: May 2006

10   9   8   7   6   5   4   3   2   1

CONTENTS

Bedtime Eyes   *1*
The Piano Player's Fingers   *65*
Jesse   *141*

BEDTIME
EYES

CHAPTER ONE

Spoon made me feel fantastic—by that I mean he made my body feel good, but not my mind. He could make love to me, but no matter how many times I tried, I couldn't make love to him. I wanted to know what other people did in the same situation, so I asked my friend Maria, but she wouldn't tell me. I wanted someone to tell me what to do, to give me a list of instructions to follow.

It took me too long to realize that it was far more difficult to lick his wounds than to suck his cock. Now I wonder why I didn't start practicing earlier.

Even now his empty bottle of Brut aftershave and his vitamin-E tablets (without which he swore he wouldn't be able to fuck) are on the counter of my bathroom sink. I can't bring myself to throw his stuff away, I can't even put it in one of the suitcases he left behind and hide it away in the back of the closet.

When Spoon ran away from the Yokosuka Naval Base, he packed all his things neatly and came to my place, bags in hand. He rang the doorbell politely before coming in, so it almost felt like I had a semipermanent houseguest staying with me. In one of his suitcases were twenty

Hershey bars he'd brought for me, but I felt strangely uneasy; it didn't seem right to accept them all just for putting him up.

The first time I saw him was at a bar on the base. For some reason he was wearing a tuxedo with a bow tie, and he looked cooler than cool among all the other guys playing pool in their jeans or overalls.

While my boyfriend was wrapped up in his pool game, a dollar bill in his cueing hand as he played, I kept stealing glances at Spoon. I remember the glass he was drinking his bourbon and 7-Up from, glittering gold, like honey dripping between his black fingers. Now when I see a glass like that it just reminds me of one of those little cups you get at the hospital for a urine sample.

His other hand was thrust deep into his trouser pocket and he seemed to be touching something. I could see from the way his hand was moving that he had long, bony fingers. He seemed to be gently caressing the lining of his pocket with his fingertips, and I blushed as I wondered how it would feel to have those same lustful fingers probing my slit, him still wearing that cool expression on his face.

The moment our eyes met, I felt as though he had read my mind, and I looked down at the floor. When I looked up again, he caught my gaze and motioned toward the door. I stood up like I was possessed, told my boyfriend I was going to the ladies' room, and left the game room. Spoon was waiting for me right outside the door, both hands thrust in his pockets now, leaning against the wall and looking like some kind of small-time gangster.

He took me by the arm and led me to a door at the very corner of the building. The sign on the door read: KEEP OUT! It was the boiler room. Inside, it smelled old and dusty, and bare pipes were sticking out everywhere.

As soon as the door closed behind us, I was alone with Spoon, the two of us in that room together.

I opened my mouth to speak. I guess Spoon took it as a sign of urgency, of my desire for him. Or maybe he simply thought there was no need to talk, I don't know, but he just forced his tongue between my lips and into my mouth. His tongue was alive with passion and clearly intent on overwhelming me.

I clawed desperately at his jacket and tore at his shirt buttons. I couldn't wait to have his scent on me. But there was no letup from his hands or his tongue, and I was so excited that I couldn't stop my hands from shaking long enough to undo the buttons. I finally gave up and ripped the shirt open.

The black skin of his chest was thickly covered with hair and he wore a gold chain around his neck.

I pressed my lips to his chest, tugging at his chest hair and enjoying the smell of his body. It was a familiar smell, one I recognized from long ago. It was both pungent and sweet, like cocoa butter. A strange smell came from under his arms, too. It was musty, not offensive, but at the same time not pleasant either. It was the kind of smell that made me aware of our primal attraction. Maybe it had the same effect that the musk of wild animals had on each other when in heat.

In contrast to my raw aggression, Spoon was quite gentle as he skillfully undressed me.

There wasn't enough room to lie down, so I stood with one leg raised high, my high-heeled foot braced against the wall, my tiny panties hanging like a handkerchief around my ankle. His black arm was twined around my leg, and the light sparkled off my anklet.

His dick wasn't the kind of disgusting, red cock that white men have, nor was it the pathetic, infantile thing of Japanese men, the kind that doesn't do a thing for you until it's inside you. With Japanese men, anyway, I always worry that I'm going to get myself tangled up in their pubic hair because it looks so much like seaweed floating on the surface of the sea.

With Spoon, maybe it was just that his pubic hair was the same color as his skin, but I was totally in awe of his dick. It was gorgeous, like a big chocolate bar, and as I stared at it excitedly I couldn't stop my mouth from watering.

We spoke only in gasps and sighs. I was too excited even to call out. In the midst of this wonderful mixture of pleasure and pain, all I could do was cling tightly to his jacket. My hand brushed against his pocket and touched whatever it was he had been caressing at the end of the pool table. It seemed to be made of metal; a familiar, everyday object . . . but then my orgasm began to build and I lost all sense of what was going on around me.

I stared at him, still standing with one leg raised high against the wall.

He brushed the hair stuck to my sweaty forehead away from my eyes, and said, "From now on I'll probably feel like jerking off whenever I think of you."

It was kind of sad to think of him masturbating with a picture of me in his mind.

"What's your name?"

"Spoon."

I remembered the cold, hard object in his pocket, and the English phrase about children born into wealthy families: "born with a silver spoon in his mouth." Friends probably nicknamed him Spoon from a mixture of affection and derision for his comical habit.

Why would anyone born with a silver spoon in their mouth want to walk around with it in their pocket? It seemed so unfair that God would make someone like him, with such a wonderful body, so unsure of himself that he couldn't help overdressing and clinging to a spoon.

"You've been sad sometimes, haven't you?"

"No, I'm always happy."

I knew he was lying.

"Come home with me," I said.

I wonder whether, at that time, I wanted to be a martyr or something. Perhaps I had some wacky idea that I could make him happy. But he soon put me right on that score.

"Put your leg down! Doesn't that make you tired? You've had it up there the whole time. If you want to fuck some more, let's do the second round between the sheets."

He winked at me the way only black guys can, one eyebrow slightly raised and his eye shut tight. It felt like a flame leaping between us. The feeling started in my mouth and settled down inside me, then gradually melted and spread, sweet and warm, throughout my whole body.

CHAPTER TWO

Maria kept pigs in her dressing room. There were lots of them and they were all really fat. There were always a few sprawled out on the tatami floor, their flabby, white legs spread wide, stuffing themselves with curry rice. Maria told me I shouldn't call them pigs, but the resemblance was striking. They were nothing like Maria at all. But I shut up about it when she told me to cut it out.

Maria walked around the dressing room in stylish slippers, wearing a black silk dressing gown. When she did her makeup, she would tie the sash around her waist, let the upper half of the dressing gown fall, and sit cross-legged, half-naked, in front of the mirror. The lining of the gown was scarlet.

"After I've done my spot, I'd like to go out for a drink. What about you, Kim? If you want to watch me onstage, go up to the lighting box and ask the guy in there to let you watch. Or would you rather wait here?"

"No, I'll watch."

Although I enjoyed being around Maria and the other Filipino dancers, chatting with them in English and swapping funny stories, I felt out of place when I was alone with all those women dressed only in their underwear, half sitting, half kneeling, sprawled out on the floor. Anyway, they were probably thinking I was out of place, too, just a kid.

Maria stubbed out a cigarette in her black ceramic ashtray and began to change into a long, white dress with a back slit running all the way up to her ass. I watched her from the corner of my eye as I moved toward the dressing room door. As I waited for Maria's turn onstage, I began to get excited—like I was the one who was going on, not her.

Of all the women milling around in the dressing room, for me she was the only one who had the ability to create a really horny atmosphere onstage. She was the only one who could drive the men wild with lust. Watching Maria onstage, swaying to the sound of blues music and spreading her legs, I was overwhelmed by the sheer presence of her pussy. Sometimes I sold mine cheap; the pitiful thing between my legs was nothing compared with Maria's—mine could never be art. Sometimes I wallowed in self-pity just thinking about it, but then I would remember the graffiti Spoon had sprayed on our bathroom wall: PUSSY IS GOD!!!

Maria came back onstage wearing nothing but high heels and a soft hat. Her supple body writhing slowly, she began her masturbation routine. Her expression was one of ecstasy, but underneath she was completely cool. I wondered what it must be like to be able to perform like that in bed. Not to be absorbed in my own feelings, but to drive a man to ecstasy. I wanted to drive the cool look out of Spoon's eyes with my own private peep show. I wanted to perform just for him, and like Maria did onstage, I wanted to push him away when he came close to me. I started to get hot with anticipation, just thinking about the next time we would make love. But I was always the one to lose myself first, and I was always the one to cry out, "I want you!"

We were beginning to get too used to each other, me and Spoon. I was always left with a sense of sweet defeat after we made love. Watching Maria perform was similar to the way I used to study for exams in the days when I still had some small hope for the future. Each time I was sure that *this* time I was going to get a good grade. But for some reason I was always so nervous when I saw the exam that my hands would shake so badly I couldn't even hold a pencil. And then my confidence would take another blow when the graded tests were returned.

"Spoon? You've picked a guy with a strange name this time. Is that his nickname?"

We were sitting at a nearby bar. Maria took a cigarette from her gold cigarette case and lit up. She carried the cigarette case with her everywhere, filling it from a can of Peace cigarettes.

"Has he got a good body, this guy?"

I looked up at her nervously—she seemed to have read my mind. She looked at me, smiling, from beneath the brim of the soft, black hat she used for her show.

"Are you going to ask me to make love to this one, too?"

I grimaced involuntarily. Which wasn't like me. Whenever I wanted a relationship with a man, I always asked her to get involved with him, too. I would have been too frightened otherwise. I'd run to her for help whenever I thought I'd found the real thing. I knew I was a bad girl, really bold, but I also knew I was a coward.

Maria always had the same quick response.

"Well, I can't."

But then she would add, "Of course, if you only need help in bed, that's no problem."

And so I would ask her to do it. It always gave me the sense of security I needed before I could love a man, but it also made me feel a little freaky to depend on her this way.

When she said it this time, though, my response surprised even me.

"Oh, my God! I've never seen you look at me like that before! Does this mean you won't be needing me this time?"

"I don't know. I'm confused. Usually whatever you say calms me down like some kind of tranquilizer, but for some reason I feel nervous this time. I don't know what's wrong. . . ."

"Well, girl, something tells me this is different—you can't even imagine me going to bed with this one, can you?"

Sure, I could imagine it. I could imagine Spoon leaving bite marks all over another woman's body the same way he did with me. But then I felt hot tears rolling down my cheeks. I was crying!

Maria brushed away my tears with her finger.

"What's all this? Crying with jealousy over something that's only in your imagination? Aren't you the sweetest thing! Come on now, Kim, don't cry—it's just a waste of time. Nothing has actually happened, right? Listen, why don't you tell me about this guy, huh? I'm really interested. Hell, if he can do *this* to you . . ."

"He's run away from the navy."

"You mean he's UA? A deserter?"

I nodded. I knew it meant I would lose him someday. He would be taken away, put in jail on the base, and then sent back to the U.S. And if he was, would I follow him, go all the way to America for him? I couldn't say. But what if I did, and then waited for his release, what then? If he was just UA, it wasn't really such a big deal—he'd probably just get kicked out of the navy. Then he could get a job, get married and have kids, and settle down with a family. Damn! What was I thinking? I couldn't imagine Spoon as a father! No way! How could his hands ever change from groping at my pussy to stroking a baby's head?!

"Jesus." I sighed.

"It seems to me like you've picked a guy with a lot of problems. He's a sailor, right? He's also a deserter. The next thing you know, he'll be living off of you."

"Don't say that. He's nothing like that. He's not weak that way."

"Is he the kind of guy who makes you feel like he's a part of you?"

"Yeah. I don't know how, but he does."

"Well, you stop worrying about what might happen then. The reason I asked if you feel like he's a part of you is 'cause that's the most important thing. You should be thinking about how you can keep what you've got—that'll put some sparkle back in your eyes."

I felt relieved. "Thanks, Maria. I love you."

"Who do you love the most? Me or Spoon?"

I was completely lost for words. For some reason I suddenly felt nervous. Maria raised her glass of gin to her lips and smiled. It was sort of a friendly little smile that didn't suit her beautiful face at all.

"I'm only joking! I just love to see the look on your face when you're confused."

She downed the gin in a single gulp, pulled on her black gloves, and stood up.

"Well, I'd better get ready for my next spot. So, anyway, you won't be needing any 'advice' from me this time, right?"

"I'm not sure . . . I might need—"

She just stood up, picked up the check, and left the bar. It was like she hadn't even heard me.

I was confused. My heart was pounding and I put my hand up to my chest to calm myself down. I had never felt so alone. It felt like the dice had been rolled and the game had already begun. But I'd never played a game as serious as this before. I picked one of Maria's cigarette stubs out of the ashtray, lit it, and inhaled hard. This brought on a violent fit of coughing; Maria's cigarettes were much stronger than what I was used to.

What the hell was going on? I was only living with him after all. It was ridiculous to get so serious about it. Absolutely ridiculous.

CHAPTER THREE

heard a key in the door and the sound of the lock turning. For the first few days it had really bothered me. Until then, I had never heard the sound of someone else unlocking the door while I was in the apartment. I just sat there, petrified, waiting for the door to open. It was such a relief when Spoon's big, black face appeared. He saw my frightened expression and looked puzzled.

"I'm not a monster," he told me seriously.

I realized just how much I loved him when he came out with things like that.

That day, he came in with a thick envelope full of papers. I was curious about what they were. The room was littered with sheet music—jazz music; I was having a hard time deciding what song I should sing at the club that night. I wondered why jazz singers always had to have that kind of low, husky voice Maria had. My problem was that my voice was soft and high-pitched. But after Spoon told me mine was the best for making love, it was enough for me that I only sounded good in bed. I quit my efforts to become a "jazz vocalist," and resigned myself to being just another singer.

"What's in the envelope?"

"It's the capital I need to make money."

"Can I see?"

But when I tried to look, Spoon just pushed me out into the kitchen and began making telephone calls. I gave up and started breaking ice to make myself a bourbon and soda.

"Oh! Shit! Gimme some goddam motherfuckin' soda, bitch!"

He turned to me as he slammed down the receiver. His four-letter words sounded so musical—to me perfect English was as boring as an impotent man drinking flat beer. And it made me feel so close to him when he called me "bitch." You see, Spoon was a bitch's man. Now that his calls were done, Spoon turned his attention to something new.

"Why don't we have ourselves a little party before you go to work?"

I stood watching in a vacant haze as Spoon carefully measured out identical lines of white powder on the cover of *Ebony* magazine and cut them with his navy ID card. I just assumed the drugs were a habit from his childhood in New York City.

"Man, my dick is nothing but trouble. He goes looking for pussy everywhere . . . in discos . . . in bars . . ."

Now he was in a good mood. Snorting coke put Spoon on an instant high, and he began babbling to a beat, his words a cross between a song and a wordy monologue. He told me it was real New York rap and that he'd been the number-one rapper where he came from. Then he told me a sad, sad story, but the rhythm he rapped it to was a happy, lively beat.

> *"When my sister was only fourteen—*
> *she was raped by my daddy and she became a mama—*
> *and that's how I learned to treat whores—*
> *and that's how I learned to fuck—*
> *but I still didn't know what kissing was then . . ."*

I stood there stupefied, watching Spoon pace around the room, and I downed my bourbon and soda in one gulp. Then I picked up the magazine and, bringing it close to my nose, I inhaled the coke in one big snort—my first time. An instant later I burst into a fit of coughing and sneezing and I couldn't breathe. I stayed crouched down on the floor, huddled and gasping for breath.

"Are you okay, baby? You're supposed to hold one side of your nose with your finger and do it more slowly. It's always tough the first time."

He was right. Everything's difficult the first time.

When I eventually stopped coughing, I looked up at him. He was looking down at me, smiling with a worried look on his face. I could see the wealth of his experience shining in his eyes, and it made me feel like a little girl again.

"I'm gonna be your teacher," he said.

He sounded so responsible and dependable. It was just crazy.

Sometimes I told Spoon he should write a book. It would be some weird how-to book about taking drugs. Or maybe about hanging out on the streets and walking like a gangster. Or maybe a teach-yourself guide to picking up innocent girls and using your body to make them crazy about you.

The next thing I knew, Spoon had got a can of spray paint from somewhere and was trying to spray something on the bathroom wall.

"Stop! We'll get thrown out of here!"

"Okay, okay."

Before I could stop him he had turned his attention from the wall to Osbourne, my cat. I saw his finger on the nozzle, and in a flash I scooped Osbourne up in my arms to save him.

At first I didn't realize what had happened, but Spoon was holding his stomach, rocking with laughter. I looked in the mirror on the desk, and discovered that I had sacrificed myself for my cat. My hair was crimson, dyed the color of a red pepper, and it stood out from my head, stiff and spiky. Even the boy in Renard's *Carrot Top* would have felt sorry for me.

Spoon was rolling on the floor now, still laughing.

"My baby's a carrot—a carrot!"

Then I imagined myself singing in the club later that night with my red lion's mane. *Oh, shit!* In my mind I could see all the drunken customers jeering at me, and the piano player trying to stifle his laughter. And then there was the manager—what if he fired me as soon as I walked into the club? If I lost my job, how would I be able to look after Spoon? Maybe I'd even be forced to let someone else use my pussy.

Spoon calmed down and looked up at me. But as soon as our eyes met he burst out laughing and began rolling around on the floor again. *Shit!* He was laughing at me. And this was all his fault! In a fury I gulped down a second bourbon and screamed, *"Fuck y-o-o-o-u!!"*

I wasn't in the habit of swearing like that. Spoon suddenly stopped laughing and stood up.

"Baby, you're turnin' into my kinda woman."

"Go to hell, you motherfucker!"

"That's right, Kim. That's the way. . . ."

Spoon inched closer and closer. I was rooted to the spot. It was like he was an animal and I was his prey. I fumbled in the sink behind me, and my hand found the sponge. I threw it at him, and it hit him in the face and fell to the floor. Osbourne scrambled around, desperately trying to get out of the way, and ran under the bed.

Without even glancing at the sponge on the floor, Spoon grabbed both my arms and pinned them to my sides. I didn't say a word. I pretended to struggle so it would turn him on, but he just pressed his lips hard to mine. I stopped resisting and fell into his arms.

Spoon lay me down on the floor and began to undress me. I pretended that I was sulking, but I wanted him to know I was only pretending, so I curled my arm around his neck, and drawing him close, I bit his earlobe. His eyes flashed, telling me he knew the game I was playing. He really was becoming my teacher.

"My darling little hot chili sauce . . ."

After we had made love on the kitchen floor, his "hot chili sauce," who was feeling quite a bit spicier, decided to call into work to say she couldn't make it to the club to sing that night because her father had died. The manager was very sympathetic and told me to take a few days off. The truth was I never knew my daddy—he left before I was born—so I didn't feel guilty at all. And what better way to spend the time than partying with Spoon? That night my stage performance took place in my room; it was a nasty little performance with a lot of alcohol, a little bit of cocaine, and just the right number of joints. And my audience was Spoon and Osbourne.

We partied long and loud, and in the end we both drank too much and threw up. By the time we had finally begun to cool down, it was already morning.

CHAPTER FOUR

I was awakened by the sound of Osbourne meowing for his break-fast. I opened the refrigerator and took out a can of cat food for him and a big carton of milk for myself. I fed the cat and then gulped the milk straight from the carton. My throat was unbearably dry and my body still felt like it was floating.

I quickly cleared away the remains of the previous night's party and went back to bed. The cold floor under my bare feet had me shivering, and the milk had chilled me through to the bone. All I wanted was to curl up under the warm blankets and go back to sleep again.

Making a gap in the venetian blind with my fingers, I peered outside. It was raining. It looked as though it wouldn't stop all day. I was feeling good and put the telephone away in the closet. When it starts raining early in the morning it feels like evening all day long.

I slipped into bed beside Spoon, wrapping the blankets around me. To me his naked body was the most comfortable sheet in the world.

"I can hear rain," he mumbled

"Are you awake?"

"Uh-huh . . ."

"It looks like it could last all day long."

"I feel like shit."

"Tired?"

Spoon stared into the big frameless mirror by the bed, and answered, "I've got a hangover."

"Me too. I think it's a good excuse to spend the day lying around."

"Umm . . ."

Resting his cheek nonchalantly on his palm, his elbow on the pillow, Spoon began caressing my body. It felt so good, my eyes narrowed like a cat's and I confessed to him, "You're my most comfortable sheet."

"Yeah? Well, you're my blanket," he said with a smile.

The way he put it made him seem so innocent, like some rough, inexperienced young boy trying to whisper sweet nothings. It reminded me of the way I was impressed by Chet Baker even though he had a terrible singing voice. Whenever I listen to his songs, my insides feel like sugar dissolving.

It was still raining. Spoon began to nibble my earlobe. I wasn't wearing earrings, so I could feel the saliva seeping through the hole in my ear.

Spoon asked me what my favorite time of day was for making love.

"Anytime," I said coyly.

He told me he liked to make love best in the morning, especially if it was raining.

"It's raining now," I reminded him.

"You didn't know that about me, did you?" he said tenderly.

He pressed his lips to my neck and sucked hard—so hard I thought he might suck the skin clean off—and he left a spider's web of purple bite marks scattered across it. Meanwhile the spider inside me was waiting to feast itself on his heart, but it wasn't long before I gave up on such an ambitious plan and began enjoying my role as Spoon's little plaything. And as he threw his toy around like some impulsive child, I began to feel pleasure in the pain.

He reached out his arm and put a record on the turntable. On days like this he liked to listen to Thelonius Monk. The piano sounded like rain. My pleasure was interrupted.

Spoon lay on the bed, his burnt-black body only partly covered by the sheets. He reminded me of Brother Rufus in the Baldwin novel, listening to the saxophone and crying out from deep down inside his heart: "Please, won't you give me your love?"

Spoon didn't need a saxophone. He could say all he wanted to say with his body. I would probably have even become an alcoholic prostitute for Spoon if he had wanted me to. But I wouldn't have wanted him to be my pimp—if I were up for sale, he wouldn't be able to leave bite marks on my neck anymore.

"When I was young and I didn't know anything about women, a friend of mine told me they had a hole between their legs for guys to stick their cocks into. So from then on I thought there was, like, this big gaping hole between a woman's legs. So the first time I slept with a woman I was really confused—I thought, Damn, this bitch ain't got no hole. I didn't realize I had to look for it."

His story made me feel more relaxed.

"So now you know, do you?"

"Sure, like this. But now I don't need to search for the holes with my fingers no more—they come looking for me. . . ."

I wanted to tell him the hole was alive. I wanted to tell him it was breathing and that if you put a mirror up close, it would mist up. I opened my mouth to tell him, but nothing came out. I often lost my voice when he was doing that to me.

"Your skin really is the color of ebony, isn't it?"

It was the saddest color in the world, and yet it was the most beautiful color I had ever seen. However suntanned I got, I could never come close to the color of Spoon's skin. If I ripped his skin, the blood would flow red from his flesh. When he made love to me, there was white liquid.

I felt his head between my legs and I was helpless. I could see the top of his head, covered thickly with hair like little coiled springs. His tongue was like some enormous snail eating up my skin, layer by layer.

I could feel his little gold earring against my thigh. It always got in the way when he was down there, but he liked to wear it because it made him look good. Small rivulets of sweat ran down from the hollow of his back to his ass. I was always wary of touching him there. I was sure that if I got my hand in between the hard muscles of his butt cheeks, he'd grip it so tight I wouldn't be able to get it out again and I'd probably have to cut it off at the wrist. It would be like the little girl in the fairy tale, the girl with the red shoes who had to keep on dancing and dancing and couldn't stop until they cut her feet off. I'd have to keep dancing, too.

I didn't want to lose these things that bound me.

"Mmm, delicious. Juicy."

Spoon wasn't concerned with what I was thinking—only with what he was feeling himself. He didn't think. He only spoke about the things his body reacted to. When he danced, it wasn't because he heard music—it was the other way around: he needed music because his body had started to dance. And now his tongue was dancing and playing music all over my body.

There was no let-up of his tongue. My pussy juices were starting to turn into the kind of filmy skin you get when you boil milk.

"Do you know how cats fuck?" he asked.

"No . . ."

In an instant I felt Spoon's weight on my back. His thick, wiry chest hair was rubbing against my spine, and I felt like I was going to cry. Then suddenly he bit my left shoulder hard.

"That hurt! What the . . . ?"

"This is the way cats fuck—till all the hair comes off the female's shoulder."

"Really?"

"Yeah, and they make a horrible noise, too."

"Like this?" I made a noise like a cat yowling. Gradually the cat's yowling gave way to my own yowling, and it gave me such pleasure to allow Spoon to subdue me. I looked in the mirror at the side of the bed. Grasping the sheet between my fingers, I could see my body laid out on the sea of white wrinkles. It looked like a blurred photograph. Then, on top of me came my favorite black sheet, forming a sharp, tight contrast. After a while I could no longer tell whether the sheets were white or black, and through a hazy semiconsciousness, all I could do was follow the reflection of my red polished nails in the mirror.

I cried out again like a cat.

"Shhh, quiet, baby. Listen to the rain."

I hadn't noticed, but Thelonius Monk had finished playing, and the rain was the only sound left in our dimly lit room.

CHAPTER FIVE

had just finished taking off my stage makeup and peeling off my big, feathery false eyelashes when Spoon came home. He stumbled around the place, shouting and bumping into things, drunk.

I got out of bed and offered him a glass of water. Not out of kindness, you understand, especially since he was drunk and being so obnoxious. I just knew how to deal with him now that we were living together.

"Drink this and sober up!"

Spoon's leather jacket reeked of cheap gin and absinthe.

"Jesus, Spoon! You stink!"

"Shut the fuck up, bitch!"

He snatched the glass from my hand and smashed it on the floor. A sliver of flying glass caught me, and blood trickled down my cheek.

"So, I smell, huh? What kinda smell? Answer me, bitch! Answer me!"

Spoon grabbed me by the neck and started to choke me.

"I . . . I'll . . . tell you . . . let . . . me go . . . I can't breathe . . ."

He tore his hands from my throat and flung me against the wall. His eyes were glassy and unfocused. He'd been doing drugs again.

"You smell like a loser, you bastard! You're nothing but one big infe-
riority complex."

He snatched a bottle of white rum from the table and threw it
against the wall. It smashed, filling the room with the sound of splinter-
ing glass and the sweet aroma of the liquor.

Then suddenly, he sat down on the floor, motionless, staring va-
cantly into space. His hands were covered in blood, cut by shards of the
broken glass. Looking closely at his face, I noticed some dried blood. So,
he'd been fighting, too. Sitting there on the floor, his fly undone, he
looked absolutely pathetic.

"Why don't you zip your fly? Did you forget to do it after you peed?
Or have you been out fucking other women?"

I knew he hadn't.

"Fucking? What makes you think I've been out fucking? You've
had some guy in here while I've been out, haven't you? You brought him
here, spread your legs and let him fuck you, didn't you, you cheap
whore! I bet you bring guys back here every time I go out, you fucking
bitch!"

Ranting and raving, he grabbed me by the hair and dragged me
around the room through the carpet of broken glass, the sharp splinters
piercing my skin.

"Is he black or white? Don't tell me he's fucking Japanese! They're
all such ugly bastards."

"You scum! You're just a no-good drunken junkie! I'm one of those
ugly Japanese bastards, too. But I'm still better than you. Dirty asshole! You
were born miserable and you'll always be fucking miserable!"

I wanted to cry to relieve the pain. I sobbed convulsively, but the
tears just wouldn't come.

Spoon just didn't have a middle ground on anything. In fact, it was
from living with him that I discovered there were actually people who
couldn't eat plain, lightly flavored food. He was altogether too sweet,

too spicy, and too greasy for that. One minute I was swimming in the sweetest of sweet cream, and the next I felt as though I'd had pepper sauce poured over my head. My stomach just couldn't cope with it. I knew I was on my way to an ulcer.

"Goddammit! Every fucker makes an ass of me! I can't do anything right," he cried.

"I can't make an ass of you—you already *are* one! I love you. Am I weird? I think you're sweet. I mean it. . . ."

Spoon stopped breathing. He just stared at me.

Shit, I thought, he's going to hit me.

I screwed my eyes shut and clenched my jaw so he wouldn't break any teeth—he had already knocked out two of them. How was it that the same hands that hurt me like this could also tickle me or take me to the very heights of ecstasy?

But he didn't hit me. He took my head in his hands and kissed me. I struggled to free myself, but he kept a tight hold on my chin. An odor filled my mouth like a virus entering my bloodstream, a mixture of marijuana and alcohol that spread and flowed through my body.

"I can feel you, Spoon."

Suddenly he pushed me away and started to throw up. It didn't look like he was going to stop, so I took him to the bathroom and stroked his back.

Tears trickled down his bloody cheeks. Spoon continued to puke even after everything in his stomach had come up and all that was left was a mixture of blood and stomach juices. I kept on stroking his back; it was like comforting someone who'd just been told he had six months to live. He cried pathetically. But what was I supposed to do? I mean, I'm not a nurse.

I took the spoon from his pocket and used it to scoop the puke up off the floor and dump it into the garbage can. I felt like I wanted to tell God about it.

"Hey, God! Look at me scooping puke up off the floor with a silver spoon!"

After I'd finished cleaning up the mess, I went to bed while Spoon washed his face. When he had finished, he came in feeling better, and in an apologetic voice he called my name. But I didn't answer. I was pretending to be asleep.

"Kim, I wanna fuck you. I suppose you don't want to do it tonight, huh?"

Fucking was all he knew. In his heart he must have been screaming, *What do you want me to do? How can I make you feel better? What else is there besides fucking?*

He was just a little, immature kid in a grown-up body. My darling Spoon. This black demon was gradually filling my mind with dirty words. But there was still some free space left. There would always be space for more until the day my mind was full and whistled like a boiling kettle.

"Kim, I wanna fuck you. I wanna make you feel good. Are you sleeping? Are you asleep? Shit! I'm doing my best to make you feel better and you won't even let me touch you."

Spoon climbed into bed beside me and turned his back on me with a sigh.

"You could always rape me."

Spoon turned back, surprised. I gave him a big grin in the dark.

He stopped being miserable.

CHAPTER SIX

had been to bed with other guys twice since me and Spoon started living together. But it had nothing at all to do with wanting to have sex with them.

Every now and then I just felt really nervous that I had let myself get so caught up in my feelings for Spoon. He was like a big jigsaw puzzle, and I didn't want to turn into one of the pieces.

One day after work I went to see a guy, an old friend. We had a very close relationship, but very relaxed—there was no pressure. We were what you might call partners in crime. In his room that night he did the same things he had always done; I thought he knew me inside out, but I left his apartment feeling defeated. Now I knew I was addicted to Spoon.

When I got back home, Spoon was sprawled out on top of the bedcovers, sleeping facedown with a glass of gin on the floor beside him. I just looked at his big, bare feet and burst into tears.

He woke up when he felt my tears falling onto his feet. I guess he thought I only cried when we made love or when he was hitting me.

"Kim? What's wrong? Why are you crying? What's the matter? Did someone hit you?"

"It's nothing."

"Did somebody do something to you?"

"No. I just missed you, that's all."

"Naturally—what do you expect?"

I didn't know what was so natural about it, but he dragged me into bed and started taking my clothes off like he was opening a bag of caramels. Then he started to run his tongue over my body, licking me all over. Suddenly his tongue stiffened. I looked down and saw with horror that there was a bright purple bruise on my chest.

Spoon was so dumbfounded that he couldn't even hit me. He held me by the shoulders, his hands trembling. I really thought he was going to kill me. I steeled myself and looked at his face. I expected to see his eyes wild with anger, but all I saw was desperation and sadness.

I had never wanted to see Spoon's eyes filled with sorrow like that. The pain was written all over his face, like on one of those teleprint signs going from left to right: "I AM SAD . . . I AM SAD . . . I AM SAD . . . "

A cold sweat broke out across my forehead. I had to do something. Spoon wasn't supposed to look like that. He was only supposed to have that nonchalant, vacant expression. I wracked my brains for something to say.

"Can't you be more careful, Spoon? If you leave marks there it means I can't wear any of my nice dresses."

"Oh, right. Last night . . . ?"

His face suddenly lit up and he pushed me down and started making passionate love to me.

Somehow I had managed to shift the blame. I never knew I could be so devious.

I sighed with a mixture of relief and pleasure as we made love, and I thought about the way Spoon's jealousy hurt him and tortured me. Whatever hurt Spoon hurt me, too. I was in love with the useless bastard!

Just the thought made me blush and I looked up at him. He stopped moving and stared back at me with a quizzical expression.

"What's the matter?"

"I think I'm in love with you. . . ."

I'm sure I must have looked really proud of myself, like I'd decided to make lobster for dinner or something.

"Naturally," he said.

I wondered if maybe me and Spoon being together was just the way it had to be. Whatever the reason, there was no question that SPOON was stamped on my heart in big, bold letters.

We were lying on the grass in the corner of a park, sharing a joint. People passed by, completely unaware, never thinking for a moment that we might be smoking marijuana. From time to time Spoon would close one eye and blow smoke at Osbourne, then roll with laughter as Osbourne just stood there, paralyzed, like it was a whiff of catnip. I was wearing a heavy coat, and was twisting the tops off one bottle of beer after another.

We were having an Indian summer. The sun was strong. When I closed my eyes, the insides of my eyelids turned into the fresh, young leaves that grow on trees at the beginning of summer. I reached out my hand and fumbled for the stiff material of Spoon's jeans. His eyelashes always tickled my cheek just before he kissed me, so I knew what he was up to. His Panama hat fell to the ground and Osbourne jumped on it and started playing with it. I wished Spoon would stop blowing my lips like he was playing a trumpet.

We stood at the bus stop in front of the park, munching hot dogs. I had put too much hot mustard on mine and it was making me cry. Osbourne was curled up inside Spoon's jacket, asleep, when I heard a woman's voice.

"Kim?"

It was Maria. I was surprised to bump into her so unexpectedly, but I didn't let it show. I just stood there, rooted to the spot, as she looked Spoon up and down. I thought I would die of embarrassment. It was humiliating to be seen with someone you love so much. Spoon, on the other hand, gave Maria a brief glance and went back to stroking Osbourne inside his jacket.

"Is this him?" she asked.

I nodded. I always counted on Maria to tell me what to do next, but I didn't want her to pass judgment on Spoon as she had my other men.

"He's a big one," she said after a moment, then mumbled good-bye, caught a cab, and was gone. I felt a little sad, like I had just split up with a boyfriend. I felt like I deserved some kind of diploma, like I had finally graduated from her or something.

The bus arrived and we got on. Spoon sat in silence while I talked.

"She taught me everything I know, the same as you have. Don't you think she's pretty?"

I winced at the triteness of my words and looked up at him.

"Not really."

I felt a moment of panic. Spoon's usual reaction to a beautiful woman was to whistle and shout obscenities at her.

"She is! Everyone says so."

"Just shut up and leave me alone."

Spoon looked out the window. His thick eyelashes were wet with tears. Now I felt sick, like I had swallowed a big lump of bread whole. The lump refused to break up—it just got bigger and bigger.

The bus jerked to a halt and the seat lurched forward violently. I gulped and swallowed the lump back down, and prayed that the driver wouldn't hit the brakes again. I was afraid that the lump would come bursting out from inside of me.

CHAPTER SEVEN

set my gaze on Spoon as I stuffed my scrambled-egg breakfast into my mouth. He had skipped his usual breakfast, a couple of aspirin washed down with Tanqueray gin, and was looking over some papers that he held carefully in his hand as he talked on the phone to some embassy or other. And every now and then he would just shut his mouth or close his eyes and stop moving.

I wanted to say, *Hey, your girl's got eyes for nothing but you,* but all I could do was sit there beside him, stealing the odd glance at his big, black face.

Spoon had told me not to play Chet Baker so early in the morning, but other than that he hadn't said a word. He was usually so loud about everything, but recently he'd been really quiet. Who'd he think he was, a philosopher or something? He had even quit snorting coke. But he smoked all day long, his big body sprawled out on the couch. Spoon worried me.

His eyes, which always told me exactly what he was thinking, were full of anxiety. And what had happened at the bus stop was still gnawing at me. What was that all about, and why was I still so upset about it?

It was as though we had reached an important point in our depraved life together, and a bookmark had been thrust in between us to mark the event.

I was picking some egg from between my teeth with a toothpick when I hit a raw nerve in a bad tooth. It made me feel so depressed. The ache in my tooth hit another nerve somewhere in my mind.

I snatched the pile of papers from the table and flung them at Spoon, but they just fanned out in perfect order in front of me like a lost poker hand, and that made me even more angry. Spoon responded with a sharp slap across my face, and I suddenly realized the papers must be some kind of plan he was working on.

I fell to the ground with the force of the blow, but Spoon gave me no more than a glance as he gathered up my cards (he had certainly won that hand) and left the apartment without a word.

Alone in the room, I crouched down and clutched my hands to my chest. Then I rolled over onto the floor and started kicking my legs in the air, screaming and crying like some spoiled child. But it didn't ease the pain in my heart. I tried calling out his name like I was just calling out the name of a kitchen implement: "Spoon!"

Just a tool for getting the food from the bowl to the mouth. I started kicking my legs in the air again.

"SPOON!"

This time I yelled like I was calling for my man, and hot tears flowed from my eyes. That made me feel a little better.

I had always stayed calm before, even when Spoon beat me half to death. Spoon and me, we were bound too close to each other and our relationship was something far too insincere to be called love. I knew there was no reason for me to worry about Maria, and that made me feel even worse because I knew I didn't need a reason—Spoon had shown me exactly how he felt, and I could see the pain in his expression. Whenever

Spoon hurt, I felt pain, too, and then neither of us could help the other because we were both hurting so badly.

On one hand, I was pleased that Spoon was attracted to Maria—at least he had good taste. But it made me feel more jealous than I had ever felt before. What an ungrateful bastard he was! How could he leave his glass before drinking the last drop? I wanted to despise him because he had no manners, but it only made me hate myself.

I had to go and look for him, so I stood up, combed my hair, and put my coat on. I wandered around town like a sleepwalker, searching for him, starting with the places he was least likely to be: the bars, the discos, and the record shops we had been to together. I even went to one of his friends' apartments where Spoon sold drugs. But I couldn't find him anywhere, so I decided to follow my instincts, and turned my steps toward Maria's apartment in Jiyugaoka. Despite the fact that he shouldn't know where she lived, like a madwoman, I was drawn there by my intuition.

I rang the doorbell, and there was no answer, but I could feel Spoon on the other side of the door begging for my help. Once, when I had been a homeless teenager, Maria had given me the key to her apartment. Now I used that key to silently unlock the door, and I pushed it open.

Spoon lay on the bed in the corner of the large, loftlike room. He half sat up. Maria's long hair, like seaweed, spread out from between his legs, and each hair seemed poised to turn into a wriggling Medusa's snake. Peeping through the hair were sharp, gold-polished fingernails.

She looked up quietly.

"Come over here, Kim."

I walked over and looked at them both lying there. Spoon's body, glistening black, looked like sweet, mouthwatering chocolate. And that was all. That was what I had been running around Tokyo like a crazy woman to find. But for me, it was worth it.

Why? Since when? Who started it? So many *w* questions came crowding up into my throat, all trying to get out at once. I could feel all those *w*'s battling it out inside me; it felt like a scene from an American cartoon. Now that was funny—I was a comic heroine! I wondered if maybe I should just throw my head back and start laughing at myself.

Maria glanced at me sideways, picked up the gown from beside her, and put it on. I just stood there, my lip curled.

"You made me do it," she said.

I just stood and stared at her. I couldn't figure out what she was trying to say. If it had been in a book with notes, I would have skipped straight to the last page for the explanation.

"This is all your fault, Kim."

She thrust the words at me as if to say, *Have you had enough? Or do you want some more?*

My lips felt dry and I tried desperately to moisten them.

"What are you talking about? I don't know what you mean. You just met me with Spoon by accident. And then, before I knew what was happening, you stole him! You conniving bitch!"

It was the first time I had ever called her a bitch. Any respect I had for her was gone.

"I didn't steal him from you."

"Yes, you did! He's *mine*!"

I suddenly realized that all of the satisfaction I got from being dominated by Spoon was actually the satisfaction of owning him.

"And you are *his,* aren't you?"

"That's right."

"Well, there you go then."

"Huh?" I was lost. She always had that effect on me.

I stared at her. Her eyes looked as heavy as if they'd had golden wine poured into them, wine that had been aged in a cellar for a hundred years. I had always been intoxicated by them; they reminded me of my own ugliness. I'd always asked her to check out the men I was seeing because I didn't think I was smart enough to judge for myself. She had taken care of me since I had been on my own, and I'd always trusted her completely.

Then, when I met Spoon, he had replaced Maria. I was too ignorant and too unsure of myself to go it alone, wavering unsteadily like seaweed in the ocean; I always needed someone to tell me what to do.

Maria stared back at me. I felt strangely calm. There was a song I used to sing about a girl whose boyfriend cheated on her. I got all worked up, imagining how she felt. The idea of her agony and her beautiful expression made me cry. She must have felt like her whole body would dissolve into tears that would just wash away. I cried tears of pity for that poor, heartbroken girl. I had never had a man stolen from me before. My love for every man I knew had snuck out the back door long before someone else could take him from me. And Maria would whisper quietly to me over and over again that that was the way things were, and eventually I would forget all about it.

Now I was the one who had been tricked, and I felt like the girl in the song, but I didn't start singing any blues. I just stood there like I was bound hand and foot, and was watching TV. It seemed like all my emotions had been frozen.

"I don't know the meaning of anything anymore. I sure don't know the meaning of love," I said.

"That's because you're in the middle of it."

What the hell was she talking about? If anyone was in the middle, it was Spoon.

I could tell he was scared by the way we were talking about it so calmly, no shouting, no fuss.

And suddenly I felt sorry for him. For the past few days he had had a look on his face like he was going to do something dangerous. But now he just looked awkward and embarrassed. So what had that serious expression been for? I was so frustrated, I felt like stamping my feet. I knew that if I asked him how he felt about all of this, he'd just say something lame like, *Hey, it's no big deal.*

But it was important to me. Even if, maybe, to this cheap whore of a man (Now how did I come up with a phrase like that?) it was just a fling.

But I had adored Maria and had even dreamed of being her lover. I didn't want to believe that an affair with her could ever be a shallow thing—I wanted it to have some deep meaning.

"You're in the middle," she repeated.

"Just lay off, will you?" I said, beginning to cry.

"Hey, baby, don't cry."

"Kim, my darling, don't cry."

Their voices overlapped.

"I love you, Kim."

I couldn't believe my ears. This woman, who I had worshiped for so long, was saying words I'd never expected to hear. But it was too late. I had already stopped loving her.

"I've always loved you. There has never been anyone else."

Now that she said it, I knew it was true. She really did love me deeply.

Far more than her hats and her rings, or her men.

"I love everything that has anything to do with you. I want to know everything there is about you. Since you've met this guy, you never come around anymore. I don't care if you leave me in a corner and forget all about me; just let me watch you. I can't bear being shut out like this. Do you know how hard it's been because I couldn't tell you how I felt?"

"Why didn't you tell me this before?"

"If I had, you would have dumped me. You're always like that. If something starts to demand your attention, you end up hating everything about it."

She was probably right, I would have ended up hating her. Especially if I'd met Spoon after hearing that.

"Besides, if I had told you, I wouldn't have been able to stop myself. I would have eaten you alive, even your bones."

I realized then that her love for me was the same as my love for Spoon. I often felt the violent urge to sink my teeth into him down to the bone.

"I wanted to satisfy my hunger with this man. I can still smell you on his penis."

I was lost for words, but Maria continued. "I'm going to just forget all about today. I'm never putting myself in this position again. And I never want to go through the embarrassment of telling someone I love them again. Next time I fall in love it will be with someone who doesn't need to be told."

Maria put her hand to her mouth to stifle her sobs. To love and to cry were equally humiliating for her. I was suddenly grateful to myself for my total lack of patience.

"Maria, Spoon doesn't belong to me. But I probably belong to him."

"What could make you say that? He's just a man, that's all. He's got nothing. Just a man. How could you?"

"He's *my* man."

She put her head in her hands and sighed. "Well, is that so important?"

"Don't forget, I don't have anything, either. I'm just a woman."

"Get out. Please, just go now."

I left them there in the room together, and left with my head spinning, full of thoughts about how we all fall crazily in love, but each in our own way.

When I got back to my place, a pang of hunger reminded me that I hadn't eaten for two whole days. I was exhausted, far too tired to cook, so I just sat down with a bowl of cereal and milk. The cornflakes got stuck in my throat.

CHAPTER EIGHT

Squatting down behind the door, I strained to hear what was going on outside. A car door slammed, and I wondered if it was Spoon coming home. The sound of a drunk kicking a garbage can. Spoon often did that, making a terrible mess all over the street. It must be him. Finally I heard the sound of the student next door rummaging in his bag for his key. He would never have guessed that a girl sat behind a door less than a meter away from where he stood, a glass gripped tightly in her nervous little hand.

A miserable feeling began to well up in the pit of my stomach, like Alka-Seltzer bubbles. I had no idea what I would say to him when I saw his face, but I knew that however much I cursed him, it wouldn't have any effect on the stupid jerk. Dirty words were just everyday language to Spoon.

I was numb with exhaustion. The next thing I heard was the sound of the key in the lock, the sound that used to frighten me so much every day. The door opened just a crack and Spoon's shameless black face came peeping through. I didn't even have the energy to stand up. I just sat there and looked at him. Spoon picked me up in his arms and kissed me, bringing in a rush of cold air from outside.

"Oh my god! Are you okay?"

He pinched my cheeks and my lips with his fingertips, playing with my face like I was a baby. I tried to explain my feelings but I couldn't find the words.

"What's wrong? Forgot how to speak English, huh?"

I tried to give him a brash smile like one I'd seen in a Jeanne Moreau movie, but I was too young to pull it off.

"Do you love me?" I asked.

Spoon didn't answer. The word "love" had no real meaning for either of us, and he usually tried to brush questions like that aside with a quick, "You know I do."

But now I could sense that the meaning of the word "love" was changing for us. It was no longer something trivial, but something dark and heavy, a word that we no longer dared use so lightly. I looked down, and removing one of my earrings, I dropped it into the glass of gin I was holding in my hand. I held the glass out to Spoon and he stared at it, a puzzled expression on his face. I pushed the glass up to the white ivories that were his teeth. It made a little clinking sound.

"Cheers!"

I forced the glass between his teeth and poured in the clear, strong liquid. The gin and the earring flowed down into his stomach. It must have burned his throat along the way.

"I hope that diamond stays inside your body forever."

Ever since then, I only wear the other earring in my left ear, all by itself.

"You know, you're *my* Linus blanket."

Spoon didn't apologize. He must have thought it was special enough that he finally knew how much he needed me, like a blanket, taking it everywhere, sucking on it for comfort, unable to sleep without it. And he must have thought that him needing me made me lucky. I just didn't have the heart to argue with the dopey bastard. He was probably right anyway.

Spoon was under my skin. We talked. We must have fucked hundreds and hundreds of times, but now for the first time we communicated with each other using words, not just our bodies. I told him how much I wanted him when he wasn't there. And I explained to him how it got so bad that I would have been happy just to catch a glimpse of one of his turds left floating in the toilet bowl. Once, I even turned the trash can upside down so I could line up his empty Michelob bottles on the table.

"Spoon, I wanted to eat your penis, to scoop it out with your spoon like I was eating a banana."

I just kept on talking. My senses were alive with sexual excitement.

Spoon looked up, clicking his tongue like he was irritated.

"Shit . . . I feel like I'm only here for you to play with. It's like your skin. When I press it with my finger, it gives. And when I take my finger away, it goes right back to the way it was."

He knew his kisses would have a much more dramatic effect on me than his fists. He had learned how to read my emotions so well that he even knew how to turn a painful bite into a deliciously pleasurable experience.

"Oh, Spoon, right now I feel like butter on hot toast."

Spoon had wanted a cat more than anything when he was a young boy. But his whole family hated cats, and no one would listen to him. He used to think about cats all the time, even at school, and he'd tell his mother about how cuddly and soft and cute they were, but she just told him that what he was describing sounded more like a girl than a cat, and that in four or five years he should try finding himself a girlfriend to look after instead.

Then one day, on his way home from a friend's house, Spoon found an abandoned cat with a bad leg. He was overjoyed and took the cat home on his bicycle. But his brothers were allergic to cats and were angry with him when they couldn't stop sneezing. In the end, Spoon decided that he would take care of the cat secretly in his bed. But it always had gunk oozing out of its eyes; it must have had some kind of disease.

Spoon's family was poor and they couldn't afford to buy extra food for the cat, so Spoon fed it his own leftovers. No one liked the cat. It was a scrawny, pathetic-looking creature, but Spoon loved it.

One morning when Spoon woke up, he found the cat had thrown up yellow puke and died; it was lying underneath him. Spoon hated the cat for dying on him without warning. He wrapped it in a plastic bag and threw it down a back alley, and as he did, he heard the echo of his mother's voice telling him, *"Cats and girls—there's very little difference."*

He was only a child, but he was convinced it was true.

My body made juice.

"Dissolve your sugar in me, Spoon."

If his dick had been an icicle, I would have melted it with the heat from my body.

"Crush me like you did the cat!"

Like that poor cat, I would remain alive in Spoon's heart and wreak my lifelong revenge. His mother was right about cats and girls.

When we made love, something about the smell would suddenly remind me of oysters, and Spoon's skin would become like hot tar and envelop my whole body. The room was pitch black. No lights. No music. Only the aroma remained. My sense of smell made me feel like a police dog, and I was sure I would be able to sniff Spoon out, no matter where he went.

He trapped me with his elbows and slowly opened his eyes to look down at his prey. He ground his teeth together. I felt like if anyone was grinding their teeth it should be me.

"I can't stand it!"

"Why?"

"You're on top of me, in control as always, and I'm trapped here underneath you, feeling like this."

"Feeling like what?"

"Like I'm gonna pass out and die."

"Open your eyes for me."

Spoon grabbed my jaw with his hand and pulled my face toward his to stop me from fainting. I wished he'd just let me pass out. That would have been a lot easier.

"I want you to watch me and feel me here on top of you right to the very end."

I started to cry. I just couldn't help myself. Now at last I understood that pleasure and pain were one and the same thing. Loving Spoon was such a painful experience. I wondered if maybe I should just wait for it to turn into pleasure. Or if one day I would just get used to it and accept the mixture of pleasure and pain.

"Look at me!"

I looked. There was no escape. I was possessed. Nothing else mattered. Everything I cared about lay between the sheets on that bed.

And maybe Spoon knew. I'm sure we would have dived into bed together, writhing passionately like worms, even if somebody had told us that today were the end of the world.

"The end of the world? Who cares?"

Not us.

I couldn't find the ashtray in the darkness, so I flicked my cigarette into a champagne glass I found lying under the bed. Then I realized that me and Spoon had never drunk champagne together. Somehow it made more sense for us to spoil a fancy glass like that than to use it the right way. And besides, we were far too lazy to make enough money to buy anything as expensive as champagne.

Savoring the taste of the cigarette smoke, I decided that Spoon knew me better than I knew myself, as though his body would be better qualified to fill out my medical reports than a doctor.

"Whenever I'm with you, Spoon, my heart pounds and my legs turn to jelly. Sometimes I'm scared you'll find out how I really feel about you."

"I feel like three stars came up on the slot machine," Spoon answered. "The bells just keep on ringing inside me."

You try to scoop up the quarters in your hands as the machine spits them out at you, but they pour out so fast you can never keep up. You feel both excited and surprised at the same time, and so happy when you exchange your quarters for a fistful of dollar bills. I thought it was a perfect way to describe our relationship.

For the first time in my life I felt lucky, like I was a winner. I felt like I could do anything, and optimistic dreams welled up inside me. I felt so good that I'm sure I would have been happy even if I were some kid going to school on a Monday morning in the middle of a rainstorm. And of course, at that moment the old gambler's saying, "Easy come, easy go," had never been farther from my mind.

CHAPTER NINE

I sat in a corner of the room where the afternoon sun came pouring in, and peeled a hard-boiled egg. A pinch of salt and a sprinkle of freshly ground black pepper and I was in heaven. Spoon and Osbourne were both sprawled out on the floor dozing, their heads resting on the magazine Spoon had been reading.

I ran my hand over the stubble on Spoon's chin with the back of my hand. He frowned a little but showed no sign of waking. He was like a big, black cat, sleeping there without a care in the world, and he looked so peaceful that it was all I could do to stop myself from saying out loud, *Please, Spoon, won't you fuck me?*

But I held back and just kept gazing at his face. I could feel a sad sense of security in my heart. I had loved Spoon so madly for the past few months, but when I thought about it, I knew absolutely nothing about my lover boy. But it didn't matter. I realized I could love no one else but Spoon, and I could only love what I knew, so I really didn't care about his background or his past. Only one thing bothered me: the file of papers he always carried around so carefully. I knew they were some kind of plans; I'd seen them that time I'd thrown them across the room at him. Then, when he hit me, I thought about getting revenge by drawing all over them with colored pencils. Poor little me . . . I just couldn't stand it when Spoon was interested in anything else but me. What would I do if he ever left me? What if he just stopped being there? Even if he was alive and well, if he wasn't with me it would be the same as if he were dead. I'm not like some girls who say they'll be happy as long as their old boyfriends are having a good time somewhere (not that I really believe them). I needed Spoon to be by my side, to laugh with and to be angry at; and I needed him to be close enough to make love at a moment's notice. If I couldn't have that, it made no difference to me whether he was alive or dead. I could only love something if it was right there in front of me. And if it wasn't right there, I never wanted to see it again—for me it did not exist.

I tried to fight it, but I had a feeling that Spoon might leave me. I wondered if the idea had come to me so I could be ready in case it really happened.

"Please don't . . ."

The words came so naturally. I tried to think whether I had ever really asked anyone for something before or not. If I had, it was for something so trivial I couldn't remember it.

I made some tea and lit a cigarette. The smell of the tea woke Spoon. The steam must have made my face look hazy to him.

"What would I do if you left me?"

"What makes you think I'll leave you?"

"I'd probably cry."

He stroked my hair. "Poor baby," he said.

"Wouldn't *you* cry?"

"I've never cried."

I wondered if I'd have to teach him how to cry, too. He didn't seem to be able to do anything without my help.

"I've gotta make a phone call."

"Who to?"

Spoon didn't answer. He just kept dialing. In my mind I told him, *I'm worried. I love you.*

But outwardly I pretended not to care. Spoon was right there in front of me. He was close enough for me to reach around from behind and unzip his jeans, then reach inside and turn him on. I calmed down. It would have been easier to love him if I lost my sight and my hearing and was only left with my sense of smell.

UA stands for "unauthorized absence" in navy lingo. In a disco full of sailors, if you were told that one of them was UA it meant that you should steer clear of him unless you had plenty of money and were thinking of keeping him as a pet. It was rare for a girl to know that a guy was UA and still fall in love the way I had. If they were caught, deserters usually had to pay enormous fines. And of course a lot of those guys, who had joined the navy because they couldn't get a job in the first place, couldn't pay, and they ended up in military jail. Even guys with minor offenses had their ID cards taken away so they couldn't leave the base. They were birds in a cage. And if they were thrown out of the navy, they just went back to hustling on the streets.

I was frightened. Not because he sold drugs, or by the telephone calls he made to some embassy, or even by the file of papers he carried around with him. The thing that frightened me was that Spoon could be taken far away from me for what he had done. If there was anything he was guilty of, it was that he had given me memories. I had never had to deal with memories before. I had always hated them and I had none prior to meeting Spoon. But now I did have memories—memories of him—and I no longer had confidence that I would be able to erase them when he walked out the door. I wondered why I was thinking about this now. It hadn't worried me a bit when all he had been to me was a helpless jerk. I had just accepted him for what he was.

One afternoon I got a strange phone call.

"Excuse me, I'm sorry to bother you. Is this an office or a company of some sort?"

"Who is this?"

"This is the Metropolitan Police."

"Are you putting me on? I get this kind of prank call all the time. Look, what do you want?"

It was no lie; every now and then some joker would phone and it really irritated me. Once it was one of Spoon's idiot friends.

"Hello, this is the navy police."

I'd started shaking, and then when I realized it was a joke I really let him have it. Poor Willie! He hadn't meant any harm.

"Okay then, give me your number—if you *can*—and I'll call you back. That way I'll know whether or not you really *are* from the police."

I dialed the number he gave me, and it was answered by the Tokyo Metropolitan Police. I spoke to the guy again, and he just asked me my name and occupation and then hung up.

I didn't understand why he had called, but at least I didn't need to worry that it had anything to do with Spoon—this guy was from the Japanese police. What did worry me was that the police might have been investigating prostitution at the club where I worked. Sometimes I got some of the hostesses to work the odd trick here and there on the side: the Taiwanese and Southeast Asian students were such amazingly hard workers, it was incredible.

I paced around the room, irritated, then poured myself half a glass of whiskey and downed it in one gulp. What would I do if the club got closed down? With my singing as bad as it was, it was difficult to imagine that any other club would take me on. I wondered if I could sell drugs with Spoon. But I was too gutless for that. I slumped down on the couch, muttering to myself.

Tina Turner was on the radio. I thought about those amazing thick lips of hers, and seeing my reflection in the dressing table mirror, I took out my red lipstick, outlined my lips with a brush to make them look twice as large as normal, and carefully filled them in. Then, over and over again, I applied kiss marks to pieces of tissue paper, and then painted on another layer of lipstick to keep the color from coming off. When I had finished, my lips looked more like chunks of ripe, red nectarine than cute little cherries, but I was satisfied with my work and lit a cigarette.

Looking in the mirror again, I decided that my T-shirt and the Levi's I was wearing didn't go well with my new lips at all, so I dragged my black silk nightgown out from under the bed and changed into it. There were claw marks in the silk, and loose threads hung from the places where Osbourne had been scratching. The whole effect made me feel like a dramatic heroine, and I let the cigarette droop from my fingers like some movie star.

The door opened. It was Spoon.

"Hi, honey!"

He stared at me in confusion, then burst out laughing.

"You look terrible! Is it Halloween or something? You look like a canned tomato!"

At first his laughter annoyed me, but then I got his joke: lips often remind people of food.

"You can eat me if you like."

He kissed me and his lips were instantly dyed red. Then he crouched down, gazing up at me intensely, and began kissing my thigh. He got some lipstick there, too. I could feel its stickiness on my leg, and as I stroked the curly hair on his head with my hand, I was almost in tears.

"Spoon . . ."

He opened his mouth as if to say something, but I never knew what.

The phone rang. It wasn't the police. It was a guy from some embassy. I was so confused that I didn't really catch the details, but it was a country with an unusual name. He asked if he could speak to Joseph Johnson. This was the first time I had ever heard Spoon's real name, and it came as a shock.

Spoon grabbed the phone. He spoke to the guy on the other end of the line for a moment, then said to him, "Everything's all right."

He replaced the receiver and turned to me with the happiest of smiles on his face.

"Baby, we've been very lucky."

But something made me feel uneasy and I couldn't return his smile. I just stood and stared at his beaming face like it was some kind of object. I couldn't even blink.

The doorbell rang and my heart missed a beat. Anxiously, I looked over at Spoon. He motioned with his eyes for me to open the door. I really didn't want anyone else to see me dressed like that, looking like a prostitute. I was almost in tears, but pulling the front of my gown together, I reluctantly opened the door.

Five people in suits stood outside. One was a dark-skinned foreign woman, two were older Japanese men, and the other two were young Americans.

One of the Japanese men spoke.

"Do you know this man?"

He showed me a photograph of Spoon. It was a terrible shot and made him look really ugly, so I didn't answer.

"I asked, *do you know him?* We know he's here."

He spoke quietly, but his tone was menacing enough to make it difficult for me to avoid his question.

"What do you want?"

He opened a small black case holding his ID card. It was attached to his jacket by a piece of cord, and as he pulled it out I could see a gun under his jacket. I was terrified. I just stood there, too frightened to speak, and they all charged past me into the apartment without even taking their shoes off.

Spoon must have known that something was wrong. He was hiding silently in the back room. But the suits were determined, and they kept searching until they found him.

I heard them struggling and then Spoon shouting angrily, "She's got nothing to do with this! Shut the door!!"

Dazed, I stood riveted in the doorway, completely dumbfounded. When I came to my senses I caught sight of myself in the mirror. My face was deathly white and the lipstick I had painted on so thickly was now double-crossing me. It made me look like I was smiling.

After a few moments the five people came out of the back room. One of the Japanese men said, "He wants to talk to you. You've got fifteen minutes. You can go in now."

I was grateful for his kindness, but I was so nervous my legs were trembling.

"Spoon . . ."

He was sitting quietly on the bed. That bed had been everything to us. He'd made me laugh and cry there. I wondered if we would ever have the chance to use it again.

It was already night. I had planned to cook ribs for him and I had already put them on the bottom shelf of the fridge to defrost. I liked to roast them in the little oven with tomatoes and red peppers to make them spicy, and add some bay leaves to bring out the flavor. Oh, and plenty of ground black pepper, of course. Spoon had never got around to buying me the garlic press I had been after, so I crushed it with a knife blade instead. Last of all I would add ginger, nutmeg, paprika, and anything else I could find in the cupboard.

As it cooked, the sticky, bloody smell of the meat would gradually change to something much more appetizing as the meat started to brown. And when the bones went a reddish-brown color and glistened with fat, I would turn off the oven and drain the fat. Then I would open a bottle of red wine, put it on the table with a pile of napkins, and call Spoon. There would usually still be a lot of grease left in the bottom of the roasting pan, fat that oozed from the ribs as they cooked, and it smelled so good, I liked to spread it on slices of toast and throw them in a basket to eat with the meat.

Spoon liked to scrape the meat off the bones with his sharp teeth. Drops of grease would fall from his lips into his wine and float on the surface in little round globules. And sometimes a few of those globules would merge together to form one large one. It was cheap, sparkling, red wine from America, and the grease and tiny bubbles mixed together in the glass made it look like it was moving.

Spoon never bothered using napkins when he ate, so his greasy fingernails shined like ripe chestnuts. By the time I was finishing my first rib, he was usually finishing the very last one on the plate, so I never got full.

"I'm still hungry," I'd say. "Let me lick your fingers."

Then, gazing into his eyes, I would suck the grease from his fingers, one by one. I would know he wanted me then. It was written all over his face. And the look in my eyes would say, *What do you want to do now, Spoon?*

Those dinners of debauchery were our greatest luxury.

"What should I do about the spareribs?"

There were tears in my eyes as I said it.

"I suppose I'd better just throw them away, huh? But it's such a waste!"

I flopped down on the floor and began sobbing my heart out.

"And I really wanted ribs tonight, too."

My mind was suddenly flooded with memories of everything we had eaten together. It was soul food, hot and spicy and full of flavor, not mild like Japanese food. Things like ham hocks, a stew made with white beans and a smoked ham shank, and okra gumbo, a spicy stew with meat so tender it just fell off the bones. Then when you sucked those bones, they were full of thick, tasty jelly. And Spoon just loved Tabasco—whenever we had fried chicken he would pour tons of it all over the dark meat. And of course chitlins—stewed pig giblets. It was the kind of food that most Japanese would never think about eating, but I was happy to eat anything with Spoon. I just thought about how the food would become part of his body, and it made me feel like I was eating part of Spoon himself.

"I shouldn't really be talking about food at a time like this, should I?"

Spoon didn't say a word. He just looked at me. His eyes were sad but there was a smile on his lips.

"You haven't said it today, Spoon."

"Haven't said what?"

"Your favorite four-letter word."

"Huh? Oh, that."

"It's not like you."

"Hmm?"

"Say it for me."

"*Fuck!*"

"Now do it to me."

He held my face in the palms of his hands. I caressed his fingers and his wrists. When he spread his fingers wide, one hand was big enough to cover my whole face. There were only three thick lines on his palms, and that made them look deceptively simple, but they were actually very sensitive and they knew every inch of my body.

"Can't we? Can't we make love anymore?"

I tried to blink away the annoying tears in my eyes, and they trickled down my cheeks and fell onto Spoon's hands.

"Our love was never anything more than just plain lust, was it?"

I stared at him in surprise. I never expected to hear such an intellectual word as "lust" coming from Spoon's mouth. It made me realize how little I knew about him, and I began to panic. I had to know more.

"There's not enough time! We're almost out of time!"

"Baby, calm down. . . ."

Spoon stroked his hand up and down the back of my neck, trying to comfort me. His fingers tapped against me, if I were the keys on an old player piano. He knew that was the best way to calm me down—it made my eyes get narrow like those of a cat about to purr. I didn't understand why anyone would want to tear us apart and destroy the happiness we had together. And the fact that I didn't know why they were doing it made it all the worse.

"If you're not here with me, Spoon, I can't love you."

And then in a whisper, I said, "I want you to be my shower so I can bathe in you forever."

Spoon spoke next.

"I said it looked bad before, but . . ."

"What?"

"That lipstick is gorgeous. You look like a real lady."

It was the first time he had ever given me a compliment, but it was so pathetic it made me feel even worse.

"You said you thought it was Halloween. I know I look like some fucking whore."

"Baby, my lady is always my whore."

It was the first time I felt any warmth in his words.

Then he kissed me.

He kissed my face all over as if, once he had started, he couldn't stop. It was as if a river had broken its banks. Unable to breathe, I just let him go on kissing me. I prayed that he would push me down on the bed and make mad, passionate love to me until I passed out from the ecstasy. But he didn't. He just held me tightly, his eyes closed, his arms wrapped around me like tangled threads. Even at a time like this, he still smelled of that wonderful Brut aftershave that drove me wild. Spoon was undoubtedly the wild brute living inside me.

And now, suddenly, he was leaving me. It had all happened so quickly. I just couldn't believe what was going on. It felt like someone was gouging a hole in my heart with a screwdriver, trying to force out a stubborn screw that was rusted in.

"Don't!"

"Don't what?"

I had seen it written somewhere, a long time ago: *2 sweet + 2 be = 4 gotten*

"Spoon, you're too sweet to be forgotten."

"Baby, you know I'm no good at math."

Sure I knew. But Spoon himself had chalked this formula on a tiny blackboard in my heart. He would probably tell me it was graffiti left there by some mischievous kid.

I sighed heavily, and as if it were some kind of signal, Spoon's arms loosened their grip and he let go of me. I knew for sure now that I would just have to give it all up. I stared at him. He had his characteristic "sulky little boy" look on his face, with his bottom lip sticking out, and I could see that he was crying. Our eyes met and he just looked at me as if to say, *So what?*

"My poor darling," I whispered, feeling more like I was his mother.

I stroked his tearstained cheeks and smiled at him. "I guess you can cry after all."

Spoon stared at the ground with an embarrassed smile on his face, not saying a word. Then he looked up and began to laugh out loud. The look in his eyes told me he knew everything there was to know about me.

He finally stood up, dropping something down between the bed and the wall as he did so. Then he turned back, and after looking at me for a few brief moments, he closed one eye and winked at me. It reminded me of that night we first met. After we had made love so hurriedly, the passion had remained and solidified inside me like some kind of capsule. Then his wink had been the catalyst for it to dissolve and take control of my heart.

Now, everything was over the moment his eye closed. I tried to hold back all the emotions welling up inside. "What are you trying to do to me?" I whispered. "You're still making eyes at me like you want to make love."

Spoon pointed at himself with his finger, then very slowly pointed at me, and nodded his head twice. I tried to tell him, *Me, too, Spoon! Me, too!* But the words just wouldn't come out.

With one detective holding each arm, Spoon left the room and left me. I was alone with no idea of what had really happened. I poured myself a glass of gin and glanced at myself in the mirror. My face was covered in lipstick.

CHAPTER TEN

ater that night one of the detectives returned to ask if Spoon
had left anything behind in the apartment—he had dropped his
ID card down by the side of the bed before they had dragged
him off. At first I told the detective I didn't know what he was talking
about, because the photograph on that ID card was the only one I had of
Spoon, and I didn't want to lose it. But then he threatened to search the
apartment, so I thought I'd better give it up. I put the ID card together
with a newspaper and Spoon's copy of *Jet* magazine, and told the detective that was all I had of Spoon's. He was pleased to have found what he
was looking for and left.

I hadn't told the detective, but along with his ID card, he had also
left his namesake lucky charm: his spoon. But I couldn't imagine the
American government arresting me for stealing a spoon.

The next day on FEN radio news, they said that Spoon had been arrested for trying to sell confidential military documents. There was
probably a big article about it in *Stars and Stripes,* too. Actually, I was
surprised to hear that Spoon had been dealing with something so
important—maybe he was more clever than I had given him credit for.
But all that meant nothing to me anymore.

For the first few days I just sat on the floor in my apartment like an idiot, staring at myself in the mirror, my face still covered in lipstick from the night Spoon had left.

Then, I finally started to come around, and I noticed that the meat in the fridge had gone bad and was beginning to smell. I opened the lid of the wastebasket to throw it away, but I got sick to my stomach and I had to run to the bathroom to throw up. Even after I'd been sick, the pukey feeling wouldn't go away, and it made me so mad that I picked up Spoon's bottle of Brut and threw it at the wall. It was made of cheap plastic, so it didn't smash. Only the top broke, and the sweet fragrance of the aftershave filled the room. As soon as it reached me, I began to cry, wailing like an animal.

At last I understood. I had lost Spoon. I cried and moaned as if I were at death's door.

"Spoon! Where are you?"

I began to search madly around the room, turning the whole apartment upside down, desperate to find something he might have left behind: sperm stains on the sheets, any sign of that bout of Philippine crabs we just couldn't get rid of when we first met. Anything would do. Anything at all. I even turned his Panama hat inside out in an effort to find even one solitary, springy hair. I found his toothbrush, and his bottle of aspirin, and when I opened the jar of Vaseline I found the traces he'd left with his fingers—he scooped it out with his big, rough fingers and used it to make me feel horny. I found the wrapping from one of his packs of cigarettes, too—he used to bite them open from the bottom— the stocking cut in half with a knot tied in the end to keep his "springs" in order, a half-eaten chocolate chip cookie, and an empty bottle of Bacardi—he didn't need a glass, he just drank it straight from the bottle. By the time I had gathered all his junk together, I was completely exhausted.

I lay down on the floor, grinding my teeth. It was over. But what was it that had ended? Was I supposed to be able to convince myself that just because I could no longer see him there in front of me, he had never existed in the first place?

I started tap-tap-tapping with the spoon. A constant stream of tears fell from my eyes, and I was afraid that my memories of him might flow out with them and be washed away and lost forever. I loved those memories. They were everything to me. I even loved the *word* "memories"! Up until now that damn word had never meant anything to me at all. In fact I had always been proud of my fantastic ability to forget. This was the very first time I had ever had anything I wanted to call my own. I wondered if maybe there was still some sperm floating around inside me. I prayed that there was, and that it would seep into every last cell, spreading its sweet smell throughout my whole body.

After a while I gave up fighting and decided just to take life as it came. Little by little my memories began to settle, sinking to the bottom of my mind, and on the surface I appeared relaxed, as if nothing had ever happened. Like smooth, calm water without a ripple to be seen. No one around me knew. And then, every once in a while, I would secretly reach in and gently scoop up some of the cream that had settled to the bottom of my mind with my fingers, and lick them. It gave me an enormous feeling of satisfaction to finally savor those memories again.

"Mmm . . . delicious!"

Let's say, for example, that there was a huge pile of hands, and that they all looked the same. I would still be able to pick out those horny, black hands of Spoon's with no problem at all.

And let's say there were loads and loads of men's asses all lined up. All the same, all with a crack running down the middle. I would still be able to spot the one that could grip my hand and not let go. And in the same ceremonial way you might choose a Filipino hooker, I would shower his butt with champagne to call him over to me.

Spoon was part of my own body now.

Now I drag my poor, weary body off to bed and turn down the blankets. I can't escape the illusion any longer—the illusion of those sharp eyes hiding there, waiting for me.

THE PIANO
PLAYER'S
FINGERS

* * *

There is always a moment when I know: when my boyfriend is putting sugar in his coffee, shaking one of those sugar dispensers with the metal spouts to get the sugar out, and then suddenly the whole top comes off and all of the sugar spills into his cup, and he sits there with a stupid grin on his face; or when I see that bottle of musk oil with the faded label—they both might have been endearing at one time, but now they don't seem to matter to me anymore. That's when I realize I've fallen in love with someone else.

That, and when the only things I want in my mouth are cigarette smoke, hard liquor, and the taste of my new guy's cum.

At first glance, love looks like some kind of terrible disease, but adults seem to develop a technique for dealing with it, like with that bitter French coffee that has too much milk in it.

The reason why everything had fallen to pieces on this occasion was because I had had too much confidence in my own technique. People will probably say it was just a love affair, and that's how I want it to be. I would rather die than let anyone know how important he was to me:

my feelings for this man made me realize just how worthless all my other memories were, as well as all of the little tricks I had learned along the way.

All I knew was that I wanted him.

CHAPTER ONE

O pen the window, D.C.!"

There was no answer.

Clouds of white steam poured out the bathroom from the half-open door and seemed to make directly for me as I lay there on the bed. I hated waking up with my eyelashes all wet and stuck together because it made me think I had been crying in my sleep. But I never had any reason to cry. Then I would realize it was that jerk D.C.'s fault for letting all the steam out into the bedroom again.

I was always yelling at him to keep the door closed when he took a shower—he usually spent over an hour in there anyway. At first he would do as I asked and close the door, but after a while the steam made him feel like he was smothering, and, struggling for air, he would open the door a crack.

Today he hadn't even bothered to ask me if it was okay, because I was asleep. He was such an asshole.

Irritated, I crawled out of bed and walked across the floorboards to the window, combing my fingers through my hair. I heard a small *snap!* and looked down at my hand—one of my fingernails was broken and a hair had caught in the split in the nail. *Dammit, D.C.!* It was probably his fault my nail was broken in the first place. It must have happened in bed the night before. The silver-polished tip was probably still buried in his shoulder. *Shit!* What a waste of a good nail.

But maybe I was being too hard on him—my fingernails were really too weak for me to grow them long, anyway.

I opened the window and looked out from the fourth-floor apartment. The sun was already high in the sky, and the May sunshine seemed to be the same temperature as my body. I was still feeling drowsy, like a pregnant cat at the end of spring, and I dropped into a chair by the window. I could feel D.C.'s sperm slowly dripping down out of me, leaving stains on my nightgown.

I turned the radio on and lit a cigarette, screwing up the empty red packet and throwing it on the floor. I knew that D.C. would pick it up and put it in the wastebasket later.

I looked down from the window and could see azaleas blooming in the flowerbed below. They were so crowded together down there that they looked like they were growing on top of one another. Both the air and the flowers were perfectly still. But then, as I watched, the warm sun on the bushes seemed to make the flowers sway a little from side to side. Strange. I stared a little harder and saw that it wasn't the sun after all.

A man was in the bushes. He was gently pulling the bright pink flowers from their stems. He deftly removed the blossoms one by one with his large fingers and then sucked the nectar from the narrow end of the trumpet-shaped petals. The way he placed each flower to his big, thick lips made him look like some kind of carnivorous plant drinking cherry brandy. He raised his eyebrows and gazed skyward. He still had one of the flowers in his mouth. Suddenly, I realized that the flower was exactly the same color my toenails had been two years earlier.

That was the time *he* had knelt down in front of me and clumsily tried to paint my toenails with that vivid, shocking-pink nail polish. He had gazed at the nails so lovingly, but he just couldn't wait for them to dry before putting them in his mouth, and it had all stuck to his lips like sticky slime. I just couldn't stop laughing—he had looked like a little boy who had eaten too many grapes. He stared down at my feet, almost in tears. He could see the imprint that his lips had left in the nail polish, and he obviously realized that he would have to start all over again from the beginning, first taking off the old nail polish, and then repainting my nails.

I looked outside again to see if the guy sucking nectar from the flowers had any traces of nail polish on his lips.

But he had gone. The flowers were once again motionless. I wondered if it had been a dream, but I knew it wasn't. I knew that the still-sweet-smelling blossoms were there, strewn naked and dying on the ground under the azaleas.

"What are you looking at?"

D.C. was standing behind me. He was big, like a bear, but he always looked so awkward, like he was embarrassed or ashamed of his size. I really felt sorry for him when he had that vulnerable look on his face, felt kind of motherly, I guess, but at the same time like I wanted to hurt him, too, so that later I could console him. You see, I liked to keep him guessing, to keep him on his toes. Sometimes I would show him all the love in the world, and then other times I would punish him, really hurt him. He was always so desperate to make me happy, but I took a lot of pleasure in destroying all his efforts, like trampling him in high heels.

It had been the same with my last boyfriend, too.

I was going over it again in my mind, dredging up old memories from the past, and the guy sucking nectar down in the azalea bushes seemed to be a part of it all. Those memories from two years earlier were much stronger than I had realized.

I always went for the same kind of guy. I liked my men big and pathetic—the kind of men I could control, the kind of men I could make deliriously happy or desperately miserable with a single glance. They were difficult to find, but once our eyes had met there was no need for conversation—they would just come running to me, sniffing around me like dogs, and they'd be only too willing to fall at my feet and place me high on a pedestal. They were the kind of men who knew that I was the only one who could make them happy.

It was two years ago that I first discovered the pleasure of owning them.

D.C. interrupted my thoughts. "Hey, Ruiko. Why don't we go to Great Fats for dinner tonight?"

"Huh? I don't want to go *there*! The meat is always so tough. And anyway, there's a new restaurant just a little further down from Fats, isn't there?"

"There is?"

"You don't know anything, do you? I want to go to the new place, okay? They have seafood."

I could tell D.C. was already trying to figure out what to wear to the new restaurant that would please me, and I went back to daydreaming about my affair two years before. *He'd* been crazy about me, too; he let me treat him like a slave.

Just then, the telephone rang, and I answered in a cheerful voice.

"Hey, Ruiko, have you heard?" It was a friend of mine.

"Heard what?"

"Leroy's back!"

"Oh yeah?"

I was surprised, but I tried not to give that away in my voice.

"I wonder if he came back to see you?"

"No way," I said offhandedly.

But as we chatted, I began to consider the potential in the situation—sure, there were plenty of things I would find annoying about him being around again. At the same time there was also plenty to look forward to—and when I put down the phone I could almost taste the excitement.

The needle jumped on the Billie Holiday record I was listening to, but I didn't even feel like shouting at D.C. I just repeated to myself what my girlfriend had told me.

Leroy Jones is back.

CHAPTER TWO

The first time I met Leroy was two years ago at a party. He was sitting behind some of my friends. They were all dressed up, but he blended into the background like part of the furniture. Compared with everyone else there—the women, who had obviously spent most of the day deciding what outfit to wear, and the gay men, determined to look their best in their sharp, well-made suits, Leroy was camouflaged—he stood out no more than the table napkins or someone's jacket casually draped over a chair.

Every now and then I stole a glance in his direction. He was sitting behind a really talkative guy I knew called T-Baby, smoking cigarettes and listening to the music with his eyes closed. Everyone at the party knew one another, but no one seemed to know where anyone else worked or what he did. The fact was, we weren't connected by our daily lives at all, only through parties—and we lived for them.

I was interested in Leroy because I couldn't understand how he came to be a part of our scene—he didn't seem to fit in with us party animals. It wasn't so much his dark skin or his extraordinarily thick lips that set him apart from the rest of us, but the hideous clothes he was wearing—his suit was a serious "World's Worst" contender. But even more striking than that, he was unshaven and kept looking around nervously. Everything about him said *hick*. And we hated people like that—he just wasn't sophisticated enough to be one of us.

When Leroy got up from his seat, I struck up a conversation with T-Baby.

"Why's he so quiet?" I asked.

"Who, Leroy? He talks with a long, Southern drawl, that's why."

So that was it. Listening to the sharp, snappy conversations everyone else was having, their fast-paced city talk laced with one-liners, it must have seemed like a foreign language to him.

Personally I kind of liked the way Southerners talked, although sometimes I couldn't understand a word of what they said because of the slow drawl of the accent. But I found it strangely erotic, as if those long, lazy words were long, lazy fingers, softly stroking my skin, gently caressing me.

"Hey, everybody, Ruiko likes Leroy!"

I squirmed with embarrassment, blushing as I tried to deny the accusation, but my protests were drowned in a frenzied sea of cheers and whistles.

Suddenly all the noise and excitement died—Leroy was back in the room. Despite the excited chatter about us—someone had even suggested cracking open a bottle of champagne to celebrate—no one seriously imagined we would get together.

After that, people kept winking at me and smiling knowingly, making sure that Leroy was looking the other way first so he wouldn't notice. Despite the sudden interest, however, no one paid any attention to him directly. Just because of the way he was dressed, no one wanted to allow him to become part of our group.

I felt a little ashamed to be part of such a stuck-up crowd, and I moved my chair over to where he was sitting. And as I did so, the topic of conversation changed to music and clothes; they soon forgot Leroy and me.

Leroy just sat there, his socks drooping down around his ankles. I was in quite a mischievous mood anyway, so, instead of starting up a conversation, I reached out with one of my red stilettos and hooked a long, sharp heel into the top of one of his socks, and gently pushed it down as far as it would go—till I could see his ankle. He looked taken aback for a few moments. Then he seemed to come to his senses and reached down quickly to pull his sock up.

I pulled it down again, the same way. After I'd done it to him four or five times, Leroy finally turned to face me squarely.

I thought that his eyes would be angry, but they were clear and untroubled.

"Why don't we go out and grab some breakfast together?" he asked calmly.

His question took me by surprise and I looked around to see if anyone else had heard him.

"Or would you say it's too early?" He paused and looked down, then looked up at me again and said, "Why don't you come over here and sit down next to me?"

So I did.

He didn't talk much, but when he tried to say something and couldn't find the right words, he'd just stop and gaze at me with those gentle eyes again. I was somehow more touched by what I saw in them—straightforward admiration—than I ever was by the flirty games of hard-to-get that our crowd loved to play.

My hair was touching his shoulder the whole time we sat together, and I felt as if each strand were alive and sucking up the sweat from his body. Leroy was smoking Marlboros and that was just something else to add to the list of things which made him look out of place: all the other black guys at the party were smoking menthols.

Leroy was terrible at making conversation, and the look on his face betrayed worry that I might be bored. But I wasn't bored at all—far from it. For one thing, I could just see the neckline of his undershirt, and I was fascinated by how white it was. He noticed that I was staring at it, and in a flush of embarrassment, he pushed it back down under his shirt collar to hide it. But I didn't like that—he hadn't asked for my permission first—so I leaned forward and pulled it back out again. As I did so, I caught his scent. It was the first time I had been so aware of how a man smelled, and I christened it Southern Black Gospel Singer. I told him, and he replied shyly, "You know, I used to be a gospel singer."

His Southern accent suddenly got the better of me—I just couldn't hold back any longer—so I leaned forward again, put both my arms around his neck, and pulled him toward me, kissing him hard on the lips.

Near dawn, I began turning over in bed, intentionally brushing against him and tempting him while I pretended to be asleep.

In the end we hadn't bothered with breakfast. We left the club and my noisy friends behind and walked through the grassy park. I was in the mood for love. Leroy was about to light another cigarette, but I pursed my lips and blew the match out before he had the chance. Then I half lay down on the ground, and as I did so, the heavy dew on the grass soaked through my silk stockings. I started to take them off but they stuck to my skin, and as I tore at them it felt as though I were peeling freshly burned skin off my legs. Finally, I pulled my skirt right up above my waist.

"Put your matches away and come over here and light *my* fire."

He spread his wrinkled jacket on the grass for us to lie on. As he made love to me, my eyes never once left his face—I wanted to see his expression change as he reached the heights of passion. From time to time he opened his eyes and saw me staring at him, but that just made him hold me tighter. I remember how he seemed excited by my body, and that just made me want him more.

I didn't reach orgasm on that first occasion, but I writhed around passionately on the grass to make him come hard, though it didn't seem necessary to make the usual faces of agonized ecstasy that I did with other men. My skin was drenched with the sweet scent of wet grass, the slippery wetness adding to our pleasure as he sucked and sipped his way over my body. Each time he let out a moan of pleasure, a wave of satisfaction came over me. I knew I held him right in the palm of my hand, and it felt good.

There was no heavy sigh of relief when he finished. I lay in silence beneath him, the only sound the distant, somehow comforting noise of the party. His body, almost darker than the night itself, seemed to blend into the midnight air, and I felt sure that if anyone had noticed us, it would be because he'd caught the moving whites of Leroy's eyes.

When Leroy finally loosened his grip on me, I reached out my finger and touched it to his sweat-soaked body, then drew it back to my lips and licked my tongue along its length, long and slow. He shook his head in surprise, almost moved to tears. Then I wrapped my arms around the thick trunk of his neck, and pulling him close, I ran the tip of my tongue slowly around the edges of his nostrils.

"Help me up," I whispered.

My hot breath caressed his nose, and Leroy screwed up his face like a small animal just before it sneezes. He looked so funny I burst out laughing.

We hurriedly dressed each other, and headed straight for his apartment, leaving my silk stockings and Leroy's book of matches behind in the grass. The stockings were covered with sperm stains and the matches had both our fingerprints on them, so it was only a matter of time before everyone would know about us.

After we got back to his place, we made love over and over, and each time after I came, I fell into a light sleep. But as I dozed, I pulled on his chest hair so Leroy really had no chance to sleep himself. Then suddenly my eyes would open and I would see him quietly watching over me, protecting me. And I felt so happy to know he was there, guarding me—so happy that I wanted him to make love to me all over again.

It was easy to get used to. All the pleasure and all the protection, for me alone.

CHAPTER THREE

The next day everyone knew about us, thanks to my friends at the party we'd run out on the night before. And everyone referred to Leroy as "poor Leroy, Ruiko's new toy." I had never really used anyone before, but they seemed to have seen through my facade and caught sight of the real me underneath.

But to be honest, I didn't care what they said. I just loved being with Leroy.

We stayed at his place the whole next day.

I didn't like going out with him much because we looked like such an odd couple. First, people would look at me admiringly, and then they'd look over at Leroy and their expression would change to one of surprise, and it made me feel impatient with him. The problem was that he just didn't look sophisticated enough to be with me. I had always been able to turn heads, but not like this, so whenever we went out together I felt so uncomfortable, I'd break out in a cold sweat. Fortunately, he usually seemed to notice and took me home so that we could be alone together.

After we'd been out, I was always in a bad mood, so I'd kick my

shoes down the length of the hallway to his apartment, then order him
to go and pick them up. I would wait for him to go and get them, leaning my head back against the wall with my chin stuck out, and like a
loyal hound, Leroy would fetch them. Then, stretching out my legs one
at a time, I would imperiously wait for him to put them back on.

After that I would usually feel a little better, and we'd start looking
for the key to the door, and as soon as we were inside and alone together,
Leroy could relax again. And because we were alone I was able to love
him again.

That sort of thing happened a lot, so after a while we came to the
conclusion that we preferred to stay in the apartment.

One day we were drinking piña coladas and watching soap operas on
TV. Leroy was sitting cross-legged on the floor and I sat leaning against
him, using him as a couch, but each time I moved, my elbows dug into
him and he jumped—sometimes when we were together he behaved
just like a little kid. He seemed to have no experience with women at all.
One thing was for sure, he had certainly never come across a woman like
me before.

I knew he wanted me—Leroy always wanted me—but I just ignored
him and kept watching the TV. Then I sensed something strange and
suddenly I turned around to see what he was doing—he had some of my
hair in his hand and he was kissing it. He saw me staring at him and
looked down, embarrassed. And I knew how much he truly loved me.

I loved certain parts of Leroy. Like the Leroy I knew in bed. I loved
the thought of his tough, shiny black body drowning in my pussy. And
I loved the miserable expression on his face when he was jealous. Of
course, his eyes and his mouth were the same eyes and mouth in the
photograph on his driver's license, but when Leroy was unhappy, a
mask of sadness dropped down over his face, and his bright eyes became
dull and his breathing got shallow and jerky. After a while I learned

how to recognize how he was feeling from even the tiniest changes in his expression.

Leroy treated me like a princess, and I loved feeling like that. To him I was fragile and precious, something to be treasured, and more than anything, that was what I wanted.

He was always so gentle with me, and when we made love he was careful to lean his weight on his elbows so as not to crush me—there was always a gap between my body and his. The gap was a very warm, comfortable space that enveloped my body. It was a quiet, relaxed place where I could rest, and I felt safe there, perfectly protected from the world outside by Leroy's body.

He worshiped me. It was so easy to control him. Somehow he managed to get some rest while I was sleeping, but I'm sure that if I had stuck false eyes on my pussy and laid there with my legs apart, he would never have been able to get any sleep.

I really used Leroy. I suppose he might have mistaken that for love, but the truth was that whenever I saw him I was consumed with a passionate rage, the same sort of feeling I had when I came across something beautiful that I could make my own: my first reaction was to destroy it. I used to smash my beautiful crystal perfume bottles on the floor. And one day I threw my rabbit-fur muffler in the bath. But when it came to my beautiful, black cat, I could never really have hurt him—I was afraid of what he might do to me in return. Maybe he would wreak some horrible revenge on me like the cat in the Edgar Allen Poe story.

I poured my glass of piña colada on the floor. It was a large glass, full to the brim, so the floor was awash with the milky-white liquid, which lay in a thick, wet pool on the shiny wooden boards. I stood up and began taking off my clothes.

The room was filled with the heady aroma of coconuts. Leroy was already drunk. I sat down, naked, on the freshly poured cool, white sheet. A sliver of ice touched my hot skin. It felt good. I looked over at Leroy. He was kneeling down, staring at me, completely fascinated. He knew what I wanted. I felt as though my skin were soaking up the sweet alcohol like blotting paper.

"Hurry, or my pussy will be full!"

Leroy clambered over to where I lay and dived headfirst into my pussy to stop her from drinking too much. I writhed on the floor, wrapping my body in the sheet, a thin, white film covering my skin, but by then I was beginning to feel drunk myself and my arms and legs felt heavy. My hair spread out on the floor around me like the long tendrils of a plant on the seabed, swaying in a warm ocean current.

Leroy must have been thirsty. He lapped at me like a dog, slurping at my skin deliciously, flicking the tip of his tongue over my electrified body, gorging himself on every last drop of the sweet, sticky liquid that covered me.

The hot afternoon sun shone down through the open window, bathing my face in its warm glow. The powerful scent of the rum was overwhelming, and I closed my eyes and let it wash over me in waves. Looking down at Leroy, my eyes half open, I could just see his forehead bobbing gently between my legs. Like an old alcoholic, my eyes filled with tears as I watched him.

Leroy stopped licking and looked up at me questioningly, his eyes begging for permission to go further. I shook my head slowly from side to side: permission denied. His tongue returned to work.

Beyond his forehead I could see his firm, round ass and it gave me a warm feeling inside. I felt as though Leroy had been put on earth solely to make me feel good. And the only reason he had been given a tongue was so that he could lick my body like this. But while I refused to let him go any further than that, I did show him some compassion: I allowed him to start jacking himself off.

The hot sun moved slowly around the room and its golden rays filtered down across Leroy's body, casting a long, dark shadow. In the apartment next door someone was playing old records and I could hear the gentle strains of "Where Is My Baby?" drifting in through the open window. I held Leroy's head in my arms.

"Your baby's here. . . ."

The sunlight painted Leroy's face scarlet. His fingers were wrapped tightly around his dick, his thick knuckles lined up in a smooth curve down the length of the shaft, and as I watched him, my pussy began to feel lonely, empty without him inside me. I felt as though she were crying to herself, whispering, *I miss you . . . ,* from between my legs. But sometimes crying can make you feel better when you're lonely.

"Leroy, you're so sweet . . . ," I panted in his ear. Thick jets of hot sperm gushed out into the coconut juice, one sticky liquid almost indistinguishable from the other.

All I could think about was pouring more rum over it and licking it all up off the floor.

CHAPTER FOUR

Leroy loved the piano. Once, just before dawn when I was walking to his place to sleep, a familiar melody drifted over from a bar nearby. The bar was closed, but I peered through a crack in the door. And there was Leroy at the piano. He saw me and motioned for me to come in, and he sat me down next to him on the piano stool and gave me a glass of hot lemonade to drink. He was humming to himself as he played, but I couldn't place the tune.

Leroy's fingers looked far too big and ungainly to play the piano. But his music moved up through the soles of my feet and I felt it on my skin. Without thinking, I held on to his arm, mesmerized by his fingers as they wove their magic spell across the keyboard. He gave me a sidelong glance without turning from the piano, then winked at me and smiled. I realized that, for the first time, he'd outwitted me.

I snatched the cigarette from his mouth and placed it between my lips. The brown filter was squashed and wet, and it had his teeth marks embedded in it.

"This is a great tune to smoke to," I said.

Leroy smiled. His hands flowed over the keys like water, his elbows thrusting, punching the air as he played. I had never seen this side of him before. Those taut, muscular arms were the same arms that held me at night, but I had never seen them move that way before. I thought to myself that if the only things left in the world were me, Leroy, and that piano, our roles would probably be reversed.

"Leroy, if you had piano wires stretched across your teeth . . ."

He stopped playing.

". . . I think I could have fallen in love with you."

Suddenly, he grabbed my arm and pulled me sharply toward him. I lost my balance and reached out to break my fall. My hand struck the keyboard, and the heavy wooden lid came crashing down onto my arm. I screamed in pain and surprise. I had never screamed in front of him before, but he just lay me down across his knees and made love to me anyway. He didn't give me a chance to resist. And with my arm still trapped under the lid, I let him.

It was only when he had finished that he realized what had happened and moved quickly to free me. I could see my red fingernails poking out from underneath the lid—the same nails I had made him paint for me the night before. My arm, now pale from lack of circulation, lay there motionless, pressed down onto the keys in one long, silent chord.

He returned the key to the guy who ran the bar and we headed back to his place together. We walked in silence. I felt as though my pussy lips had wet tissue paper between them, tissue that had been used to wipe down a very dry musical instrument. Because of that, every now and then I stumbled a little and Leroy had to support me.

He looked at me with a worried expression, his bright, piercing eyes shining into mine, and I had to turn my face away. His shirt was stained red, but I couldn't decide if it was blood from when I had bitten his neck or lipstick from when I had kissed him.

Leroy drew me toward him and held me tightly in the dark alley.

"Please, Ruiko, I need you to love me," he whispered. The words seemed to explode into the dark silence.

Wrapped in his arms, I drowned myself in the strong, musky scent of his body, powerful and heavy like the aroma of bay leaves in a rich chitterling stew. And I knew we didn't have long left together.

A short while later I stopped going to Leroy's apartment altogether. I went back to partying with my boisterous friends and staying out all night. We weren't satisfied with what Tokyo had to offer, so we often went to a club on the base, and sometimes I even saw Leroy there, too. But we didn't speak.

One night he was staring at me and my friends from across the room, but he didn't come over. He just sat slumped at the bar drinking rum and Coke, staring into his glass, deep in thought. He didn't speak to anyone. The only time he really looked at me was when I was sitting on another guy's knee, laughing loudly and drawing attention to myself, and then he just turned his head slightly and looked at me from over his shoulder. I could see the critical look in his eyes and it made me feel very small and self-conscious, like I'd been caught stripping or something, but I pretended not to notice and covered the guy's cheeks in thick lipstick kisses. Leroy stood up and stormed out of the club, kicking his way through some chairs as he left. It was such a relief when he'd gone—I felt free again.

All I wanted to do that night was to get drunk and get laid. I didn't care where I slept, and I didn't care who with. I was with the guy whose knee I had been sitting on earlier, and as we walked along the bar-lined street, I suddenly had a horrible feeling—almost a premonition. I could hear the familiar sound of a piano coming from one of the bars, and I quickened my pace as we approached. I tried to get the guy I was with to walk faster, too, but he was even drunker than I was and he couldn't stumble along any faster.

Suddenly the door of the bar burst open. Leroy stood there motionless, silhouetted in the doorway.

"Yo, man . . . ," the drunk guy slurred.

Leroy glanced over at him and then looked at me. Then he drew back his fist and punched the guy hard in the face, sending him reeling, his arms and legs flailing wildly, into the doorway of a shop across the street. He hit the door with a loud thud and fell in a drunken heap, knocked out cold.

I was frightened that Leroy might hit me, too, but he just stood there staring at me hesitantly.

"I don't want to walk," I told him, and he picked me up and carried me to his car.

Once inside I was enveloped by a strange sense of relief. I looked in the rearview mirror, thinking that the guy I had been walking with might be chasing after us. But all I could see was the crisscross lattice of the wire mesh as we drove through the gate and off the base.

CHAPTER FIVE

'm not sure what I wanted to prove that night. I turned my chair around the wrong way and sat facing him, straddled across the seat with my legs wide open, my pussy hidden by the back of the chair. Then, leaning my elbows on the backrest, I ordered him to get undressed.

Without taking his eyes off me, Leroy slowly began unbuttoning his shirt. When his fingers reached his zipper I motioned for him to come closer and he shuffled forward on his knees. He was at perfect kissing height. He didn't look at all embarrassed or uncomfortable with the situation, more like a child obediently waiting for my next command.

I spat hard in his face. That was the command I had been making him wait for. Leroy frowned, a confused look in his eyes, but in an instant his face returned to its placid, innocent self. I spat at him again. Then, quickly reaching out my hand to his half-zipped fly, I wrenched down the zipper. He wasn't wearing any underwear. His zipper gaped wide like some cheap whore's pussy and I felt bile rising in my throat; I was nauseated with jealousy.

I stood up and turned the chair around to face him, and sat back down again. Then, slowly, I opened my legs. Like Leroy, I wasn't wearing any underwear—I didn't like it when my panty line showed through my clothes, so the only things I had on under my tight, black skirt were the scarlet garters holding up my stockings.

I made Leroy sit on his knees on the floor in front of me. Then, reaching out my leg toward him, with one long, sharp, red heel, I stood on the soft, limp creature between his legs. His face screwed up tight in pain. But the creature came to life, growing as rapidly as if it had just been fed.

I pulled Leroy's head toward my skirt and put my legs up over his shoulders so we wouldn't look like some weird, hermaphrodite monster. The chair squeaked as it rocked backward and forward, and I gripped his neck tightly between my legs and threw my head back. My stilettos dug into his back and fell to the floor—I was reminded of those coin-operated horse rides that I used to cry and beg my mom to let me go on when I was small. Now I had my own horse and I could ride it as often as I liked, not paying with coins, but with my eyes, my teeth, and my lips.

I buried my fingers deep in his thick, wiry hair, and arched my back like a cat, my body stretched taut like a spring, moving up and down, up and down, as his tongue lapped deliciously over me.

But I wasn't ready to come yet, so I clenched my fists in his hair and pulled his head up with both hands to stop his tongue. Leroy just gazed up at me with that guiltless expression of his. He must have known how much that look in his eyes excited me.

I pushed him away and peeled off one of my silk stockings. Then I tied it tightly around his wrists. I doubt whether I needed to have bothered—he would never have tried to resist me. He would have hand-cuffed himself if I had asked him.

Now it was his turn to writhe. My lips melted like hot crayons on his skin, and the tight, black canvas did not resist. My long hair wandered on its own over his body as my head moved to and fro, and before long I had him crying out.

"Give it to me," he begged.

I looked up at his contorted face, the sadness and pain in his eyes bringing a lump to my throat, and I gave it to him.

Leroy called my pussy his toothless, hungry woman. And he was right—that night it was ravenous, and I was desperate to fill it. It had always seemed that I could never shake the feeling of impatience gnawing away inside me, like the brush in a bottle of nail polish, always too short to reach the bottom. But that night I really tried for the first time, and the brush finally touched the bottom of the bottle. Hot tears poured down my cheeks.

The next thing I remember I was straddled on top of Leroy's body like a little girl. He slowly sat up and put his tied-up arms over my head. It felt like a noose as he brought them down to my neck and drew my face toward his. I could feel my own black stocking rubbing up against the nape of my neck. Leaning his head to one side, he kissed me, and I fell onto his chest as though I had fainted, and took my punishment.

That was the last time I saw Leroy. I heard rumors around town that he had been looking for me, and that he was often to be found drunk, crying in bars. But no one would give him my address or my telephone number.

I spent my nights alone in my apartment, just staring into space, and by the time I started going out again, Leroy had quit the military and gone back to the States. But by then I had a new boyfriend anyway.

CHAPTER SIX

No one seemed surprised that Leroy was back. It had been two years since he left Japan, but nobody thought anything much about it when he returned. In a way it was such a small thing—the number of quiet, black men in town had increased by one. None of the people who remembered Leroy had even seen him yet. Even if they had, they probably wouldn't have recognized him.

One afternoon, I sat in the apartment, rolling his name around in my mouth. *Leroy.* It tasted like one of those sugarcoated pills the doctor gives you—nice at first, but it begins to taste bitter if you keep it in your mouth too long without swallowing. In spite of that, the two years he had been away had given me the chance to distance myself from his memory, and now that he was back again, I thought I deserved the chance to have some more fun with him. And of course, it was Leroy's duty to let me. I began to feel restless just thinking about that bitter flavor that only I could taste. When I began to recall the way things had been between me and Leroy, and considered the possibility of picking up where we had left off, I began to feel horny and excited. I lit a cigarette to calm myself down, but D.C. seemed to have already noticed my change of mood and was looking at me suspiciously.

Memories suddenly began to flood back . . . the smell of wet grass; the echo of our passionate sighs breaking the silence; Leroy's silhouetted figure standing in the dark kitchen in front of his opened refrigerator, getting himself a beer; the quizzical expression on his face when he was eating fish and realized he could still smell my musky scent on his fingers.

My heart sped up. I remembered the man who had been sucking nectar from the flowers under the window the day I got the telephone call about Leroy, and, although it was unlikely, I wondered if it could have been him down there in the bushes. But I would have known him if it were. The image of his face was burnt so deeply into my mind that I would have recognized him anywhere. And anyway, if it really had been Leroy, he would have recognized me, too, leaning out the window. And no matter how far away he had been, his dark, piercing eyes and his thick, black lashes would have blazed with passion, screaming out that he still wanted me. It wasn't that I was being conceited. That's the way our relationship was. When we were together, we just slipped naturally into our assigned roles. So I knew the guy in the bushes couldn't have been him.

"What are you wearing tonight, Ruiko?" D.C.'s voice pulled me back from my daydreams.

"Huh? Tonight? Why, what's happening tonight?"

"Oh, shit! You're kidding me, right? It's the Black Ball tonight."

I had forgotten all about it. It was just a bunch of young people having dinner together, pretending to be sophisticated for the evening, but everyone took a partner and you never knew what might happen—you might even find yourself sitting at the same table as a guy you had once slept with, who had brought his new girlfriend with him. I knew because it had happened to me once. He and I spent the whole evening trying to stifle our laughter, pretending not to know each other so the people we had come with wouldn't notice anything was wrong. And when our feet touched under the white linen tablecloth, I pretended to cough, spluttering into my champagne to hide my giggles. Actually, I had really enjoyed myself that night. It had been a lot of fun.

I never imagined that I would bump into Leroy at the ball. I wanted another taste of that relationship of ours, which only the two of us could understand, but I never wanted to hear his piano-playing again. For the past two years I had been so frightened by the memory of his piano-playing that at times it felt as though I'd built my new life around that mixture of hatred and fear.

By the time we got to the ball and handed in our tickets at the reception, most people had already started eating.

I was wearing a skintight red dress, so tight that D.C. couldn't even squeeze his hand inside. I often wore red when I went out, and after a while it sort of became my signature color, so that when a guy saw something red it would remind him of me. My red stilettos were a good example. I had worn them during so many encounters that just the sight of them was bound to make any number of faces turn red.

We washed our meal down with expensive brandy, and while we were eating I leaned close to D.C. and pulled his ear down to my lips.

"I want to fuck you," I whispered, just to get him going.

His eyes flashed wide in surprise.

On the stage, a black woman was singing a recent hit, "Somebody Else's Guy," and I led D.C. onto the dance floor, feeling the eyes of all the men in the room on me. D.C. kept up a constant lookout for guys making passes at me. He wasn't that smart, but at times like this he was my knight in shining armor. It made me feel great.

There was a guy dancing behind me whose elbows kept digging into my back, so I turned my head slightly to see him out of the corner of my eye. I could just glimpse the bottom of his tux jacket—he seemed quite tall. His gold watch peeping out from beneath his starched, white cuffs was catching the light as he danced, and half intrigued, I turned around to get a better look at him.

When I did, he was already standing there facing me, looking directly at me. He had wavy hair, slicked back with gel, and a single gold earring in his left ear. It took me a few moments to recognize him, but the suave, smartly dressed lady-killer standing in front of me was Leroy. I was stunned. Then, without a word, he turned around again and continued dancing. *Dancing!* I couldn't believe it. Leroy had always had two left feet and his dancing had been even worse than his pickup lines. I couldn't imagine anything more ridiculous than seeing Leroy dance. But this guy was far from ridiculous, and with his arm wrapped around his partner's waist, his feet seemed to move on air, like he was born to dance.

I was sick with shock and tried to drag D.C. away by the arm, but then Leroy turned back around again and spoke.

"Your stiletto heels have worn down pretty thin, haven't they?" he said in a dry, sarcastic tone.

His voice was so low that only I could hear him, and I flushed with embarrassment, the blood pounding hard in my head, making me feel faint. But my embarrassment then turned to anger, and as the blood drained rapidly from my face, I went pale with fury.

Unsuspecting D.C. half carried me to my seat, worrying that I might be anemic. I sat there pale and shivering, and when he handed me a brandy I downed it in a single gulp, the fiery liquid slipping easily down my throat. Then I took a deep breath and turned my attention back to Leroy.

He was leaning against the wall with his arms folded, a small cocktail glass in his hand, sparkling like a jewel in the light. I watched with irritation as his fingers toyed with it nonchalantly and he smiled and chatted casually to the steady stream of girls who came up to him. His neck was no longer thick and oxlike—it was far more slender and re-fined now. And I didn't once see him lean forward to talk to any of the women who came over to him—they were the ones making all the ef-fort, craning their necks to look up at him.

One of the girls kissed his cheek, and I could see Leroy staring at me through her hair. With his arms spread wide and a glass in his hand, he looked supremely confident and happy. But his eyes were cold. He smiled at me sarcastically, the corners of his mouth curling up into his cheeks.

At that moment I decided to forget all about him. I'd forget our past and if I saw him again, I'd see him as the complete stranger he was now. It was a relief, having made the decision, but I hated him for forcing me to make it.

"Do you know Leroy Jones?" asked D.C.

I was startled by his question and just stared back at him, surprised. How could he possibly know about our relationship?

"What? How do you know Leroy?"

"Are you kidding me? Everyone knows Leroy Jo ... ahh, wait a minute. You only listen to old jazz, don't you? Well, let me tell you, Leroy's the best young jazz pianist there is. I wonder why he's here? I've heard he was stationed at the base here in Tokyo when he was in the military, so maybe that has something to do with it. . . . Oh man, what a great chance. Do you know him? Can you introduce me?"

"D.C.! You can be so clueless sometimes. . . ."

"Huh?"

"What's he doing in Japan, anyway?"

"Well, an article in *Ebony* said he's here for a couple of months on vacation. He can probably afford it, too. Musicians like him are loaded unless they get into drugs or something. Must be great to be a success."

"Success? Big deal!"

"Huh?"

I remembered him fucking me by the piano; he must have figured out that he could move other people the way he had me.

I looked over at Leroy again. He had confidence now. He no longer looked up to people or turned away when they looked him in the eye, and I knew I would never be able to treat him the same way I used to, crushing him like the pig's ears in a hot head cheese.

"C'mon, D.C., let's go get some soul food."

"What? You're *still* hungry?" he groaned.

Muttering to himself under his breath, D.C. followed me out into the night. After all, he was black, and black guys can't resist soul food.

We ate in silence. The food was rich and pungent, and I remembered how Leroy used to smell exactly the same way. But somehow I didn't think he would smell like that anymore. The guy at the ball wasn't the same Leroy I had known.

CHAPTER SEVEN

For the next few days we stayed in my apartment and all we did was fuck. D.C. couldn't believe his luck—I couldn't get enough. I just wanted more and more, and eventually his dick began to sound like a fountain pen sucking ink up from a bottle as it plunged in and out. But, while my body may have been going wild with passion, my mind was somewhere else entirely.

Finally I spat out, "What's the point in all this fucking?!" and D.C.'s face took on a hurt expression.

I sat there sulking for a while, and eventually D.C. decided to take me out to cheer me up. My skin felt tight because I hadn't worn makeup for a while, but it wasn't long before the neon signs and the taste of strong liquor began to put the color back into my cheeks.

We went to a club where my friends hung out, and as we walked through the door they cheered. We all talked and laughed together, our conversation a grab bag of cynical criticisms and dirty jokes, but it made me realize just how much I loved laughing at life. If all I had to do was talk, drink, and fuck, I knew I could be happy forever.

Suddenly the atmosphere in the club changed and everyone's eyes moved to the door. I knew what had happened, and I knew I'd rather die than turn around.

Leroy was with a girl. He pulled a chair over for her and she looked up at him coyly as she sat down. She was nothing special—there were plenty of other girls just like her all over Tokyo. All she had was her beauty and her fake vulnerability.

Leroy must have recognized my group, but he pretended not to. He was wearing his tuxedo again, but this time he was dressed down, with white sneakers and a black hat perched on his head at an angle. We used "dressed down" to describe people who could look great even dressed casually, and while nobody said anything, we were all thinking the same thing—Leroy looked great.

"Who imagined that Leroy would come back looking like that?" said Roscoe, speaking for everyone.

Leroy and the girl sat chatting and laughing together.

"Yeah, who would have thought he'd turn out like that? When he was with Ruiko he looked fresh off the plantation."

D.C.'s eyes widened. *Shit!* Roscoe and his big-mouthed friends had really messed things up for me this time.

"No way! Ruiko was Leroy's girl?"

He seemed genuinely impressed, but Roscoe cut in sharply to correct him.

"You got it backward," he said sarcastically, pushing his finger into D.C.'s forehead, "Leroy was Ruiko's guy. Two years ago he was so uncool no one would have anything to do with him, but Ruiko picked him for the hell of it."

D.C. stared at me with renewed respect. He didn't have enough brains to realize that he should feel jealous. He just figured that Leroy had become a success after leaving the military.

"Did anyone know he played the piano?"

"Nah . . ."

I knew. In my mind I was screaming, *I knew! I knew he could play!* But I said nothing. I wanted them to think that as far as I was concerned, Leroy's and my relationship had just been a passing thing. So I kept quiet. And because I wouldn't say a word, they started teasing D.C. about me and Leroy. Poor D.C.: he was a good-looking guy, but not too bright.

Leroy stole a glance over in my direction once in a while, and though I had my back turned to him, I could feel his eyes burning into the back of my head. It was as though my whole body had become sensitized to his intense stare, and I could feel it getting hotter and hotter, like when you try to burn holes in a piece of paper using a magnifying glass to focus the sun's rays. When I couldn't put up with it any longer, I stood up, asked my friends to look after D.C., and left the club.

I wandered the streets aimlessly. I didn't know why I was crying, but I couldn't stop the tears pouring down my cheeks. I felt like a little girl who wanted to run home and tell her mother that someone had picked on her at school.

A car stopped beside me. I thought it must have been a cabdriver picking up a fare, but when I turned around to look, it was Leroy, his sharp eyes piercing the darkness, and I turned and ran. He put his head out the window and shouted, "You look like a hooker walking around on your own like that!"

Wiping the tears from my eyes with the back of my hand, I stopped and turned. The car drew up slowly and he opened the door for me to get inside. I stood motionless with my hands in my pockets, so he grabbed hold of my arm and dragged me into the car before I had the chance to run away again, and we sped away into the night.

It was drizzling and the road was wet. I didn't have the strength to fight him any longer, and I just sat there, thinking vaguely that it looked like the beginning of a rainy spring. Each time his foot hit the brake Leroy turned to look hard at me, and there was nothing I could do but return his stare. Then, as he accelerated, he'd refocus on the road, and I wouldn't know where to look, so I just stared at his hands gripping the wheel. His knuckles seemed much bigger than before. Now he really did have a piano player's fingers.

We drove for a long time and the rain started to get stronger, bouncing hard off the windshield. It didn't occur to me to question where we were going or to wonder what he was thinking, because I was conscious only of Leroy himself, sitting there next to me. His back was straight up against the seat, calm and relaxed despite the speed at which he was driving, and the only noise was the short gold chain in his ear making a faint metallic sound as it swayed from side to side.

I knew the guy sitting next to me in the sharp clothes was Leroy, but he didn't look the same at all, and I wondered how it was possible to create such a completely different person out of the same raw materials. I wasn't conceited enough to think that he had changed just to get back at me—we had only spent a very short time together. And even if I'd managed to have such a strong influence on him, Leroy was acting too naturally to give that impression. He looked so cool, as if he was just giving a ride to some girl he had passed on the road. And that hurt. If he'd acted like he hated me, I would have been bitter, but it would have left me my pride. Even though I was the one who had discovered his talent, I sensed that there was some other woman who had helped him realize he had it.

Leroy pretended to reach out his hand to the gearshift and grabbed my hand. But his eyes stayed on the road—he didn't seem to think it was necessary to look at me. I felt as though there were lumps of ice behind my eyes and they were about to melt and pour out. Everything was blurred but I couldn't blame it on the rain—all the windows were closed.

I was still trying to hold back my tears when I realized that Leroy had stopped the car. We were parked somewhere dark and he was leaning over me.

For the first time in two years, Leroy's face was close enough to mine that I could feel his breath on my skin. His face was the same as before, but his eyes were completely different. I thought that he would try to kiss me and start making love to me immediately, but he didn't. He continued staring at me, trying to despise me, but I could see from his eyes how determined he was to have me, too. He had only ever fucked me once before without first asking my permission, but that time I hadn't had to watch his eyes as he mentally licked his chops.

Shaking with fear I turned my face away from him. But Leroy was too quick for me—he seemed to anticipate my move, and began kissing me passionately, taking my breath away.

"I've been waiting for this moment for a long time," he told me.

But there was no warmth in his voice, and it didn't sound as though he intended this to be the start of a romantic affair. He pressed his lips to my ear and injected a hot stream of saliva, then motioned me toward the backseat of the car. Aroused, his kiss having dissolved my resistance, I obeyed and slid into the back. He got out of the car and, in the seconds before he got back in, I told myself that this was something that had to happen.

Leroy got into the back and once more gathered me into his arms, but as we moved about in the cramped space my head banged against the door. Droplets of rain sparkled on his skin in the soft half-light and he noticed some on my face, too, and although it was June, he turned the heater on.

Normally when I was smothered in the powerful scent of a man, my fingers would get to work almost reflexively, rapidly undoing his shirt buttons, but right now both my hands were balled into tight fists. Leroy pried my fingers open, one by one, and pressed his lips to the palms of my hands. I couldn't bear to watch, and shut my eyes tight, only to feel his lips move on to my neck. His stubbly chin, spiky, like an unmown lawn, used to scratch my face painfully, but now it felt more like sandpaper, gently smoothing down the skin on my cheeks.

Who *is* this? I thought.

Leroy kissed me hard, forcing his tongue between my lips, exposing my teeth like he was pushing pills from a foil strip. I could have bitten off his tongue right there—he wasn't going to use it to worship my body anymore, anyway. His tongue was hungry now, only licking my skin to satisfy that hunger, taking my moans and sighs as his nutrition.

A car sped past, splashing water up from a puddle in the road. No one knew I was being sacrificed in the confines of the backseat of this car. He pulled down the zipper on my dress.

"No . . . ," I said in a small voice. But he wasn't listening.

His fingers burned as they touched my bare skin, and I cried out helplessly.

"You've won!" I told him. "It's over!"

But for Leroy it was just beginning. The car seat squeaked as his fingers moved freely over my body—I was his keyboard. But he no longer thrashed at the keys—he stroked them so gently that I could almost feel his fingertips before they reached my skin. He had the same magic touch I recalled from two years ago, and I moaned deeply in acquiescence. Leroy's memory of my body was flawless.

He put his hand around the back of my neck and pulled me up. I knew that the thing I had feared most and tried to push away had grown over time, and was now about to devour me. I could never have imagined that something I had been so frightened of for so long would be so sweet, and I sobbed at my defeat. I had been terrified of the power in the sound of his piano-playing, but now I was being invaded by its melody.

"You'd like to try to escape, wouldn't you, Ruiko?"

His voice was calm.

"You'd like to run away, back to your slaves, wouldn't you? So they can look after you, lick your wounds, and kiss your hurts away? Well, I'm telling you now, this is just a *fuck*. It means nothing to me. So if you want to run, you'd better do it now."

But he had already driven the stake through my heart. What good would it do to try to run away? Leroy coming back had been a miracle. And now he had become the same guy who had made love to me by the piano. Another miracle. But unless I got a third miracle, a miracle of my own, there was really no point in trying to run away—there was no chance of escape.

"What for? What would change if I ran? Everything already *has* changed."

A thin smile appeared on his face. Apparently I was cleverer than he'd thought.

"You wouldn't believe how much more they still can change."

"You want to despise me, right? If you think fucking me will work, go ahead and try. I'm just about to come, you know. If you think by being able to make me *come* you can despise me, go ahead and try. But you'd better hurry."

Leroy shot sperm out over my body, like he was spitting out mouthfuls of saliva. The only difference was that when I had spat on Leroy, he had enjoyed it. There was no pleasure in this for me.

He put his arm under my back and lifted me up so that we were face-to-face. We stared closely at each other, looking for battle scars, both of us hoping to see signs of defeat in the other's eyes. I frowned and lowered my eyes first; I was the loser.

Leroy placed his tuxedo jacket around my shoulders to cover my naked body. I shivered as the cool, silky lining touched my skin. Then he put his arm around me and pulled me close, the tattered remnants of his bow tie hanging lifeless around his neck, tapping my shoulder lightly like a black, silk pendulum. Over his shoulder I could see the window, misted up with condensation.

"Would you turn off the heater?"

He turned it off and switched on the radio. An old O.V. Wright tune was playing. He was singing about how his lover was always on his mind, and that if she ever stopped loving him, he couldn't go on living.

I wiped my tears on his shoulder and reached out my hand to write on the misty glass. But then I let it fall again.

"What were you going to write?" Leroy asked.

"P-A-S-T."

"The past means nothing," he told me.

"I'd like to believe that."

Dawn began to break. It was still raining. It was probably going to rain all day. It felt cold for June, and Leroy's body no longer warmed mine. Things were different now. But he would still keep playing the piano. That's all he ever did. Even when there was no piano in front of him.

CHAPTER EIGHT

I put a thermometer in my mouth to check my temperature. I had a fever. I had got out of Leroy's car partway home and walked the rest of the way in the rain, so now I had a cold. When I opened the door of the apartment, D.C. was dumbfounded to see me standing there with my hair dripping wet. I stared back, but my gaze went straight through him.

He wrapped me in a towel and guided me to the bedroom, then went to the kitchen to open a can and make hot soup for me. I wanted a cigarette but mine were too damp to light, so D.C. offered me the one he was smoking. I was grateful for his kindness.

"I love you." I smiled.

I made it a rule never to tell lies to avoid hurting someone's feelings, and it felt the same as when I pretended I wanted to fuck even though I really didn't. D.C. stared at me in surprise, pinching himself to make sure he wasn't hearing things. He didn't even notice the soup pan boiling over. And of course, he didn't hear me apologizing silently to him in my heart.

I pretended to be much worse than I really was and spent the whole day on my back, trying to think of anything but Leroy. But he was hiding behind my eyelids, and as soon as I closed my eyes his face appeared,

enveloping my mind as if he had been waiting for me, so I had to keep
my eyes open to avoid him. I found I could shut him out by concentrating on D.C.'s smile and the things in the room around me, but little by
little my concentration would lapse until I could hear the name *Leroy*
screaming out from every pore of my body, and my mind was swamped
by a flood of memories of the touch of his hands, his feet, his tongue,
and his dick. Then, when I tried to escape into sleep, his fingers would
seize my body, tickling me and confusing me. When I woke, my whole
body would be drenched in a sweet, passion-soaked sweat, an ironic sort
of wet dream.

D.C. was sincerely concerned because I wasn't pushing him around
the way I usually did.

"You're freaking me out. I've never seen you like this before. Why
aren't you drinking the juice I made you?"

"Leave me alone. I can't even look at that juice unless I'm starving."

D.C. tried cooking dishes made with liver and kidney to give me vi-
tamins and iron, but just looking at them made me feel sick. I only
wanted one thing. I felt like a young girl again. My whole lovesick body
was weeping quietly to itself.

"You really don't give a shit about me, do you?"

Apparently D.C. had been talking about the weather and I hadn't
replied. *The weather?* That was the last thing on my mind.

"Goddamn it, D.C.! Why do I have to talk about the fucking
weather with you?"

"You said you loved me. But I can tell you don't."

I was too fed up for words.

"So if I listen to you go on about the weather, *that* proves I love you?"

"Yeah," said D.C., breaking down in tears.

It wasn't the first time I'd seen a man cry, so I wasn't particularly
moved.

"All right," I said, "come over here and hold me. That'll make you feel better."

It was the easiest way to stop his crying. Anybody would start complaining if he couldn't touch the person he loved. I used to purposely push my boyfriends away whenever they'd get like this, but I didn't have the energy right now.

As I lay in his arms, I tried to pretend it was actually Leroy who was making love to me. But my imagination wouldn't stretch that far. I knew Leroy's touch far too well to fool my senses into thinking it was him.

Leroy and I crossed paths a few times after that rainy night. He was always with a beautiful young woman and I was always with D.C. or some of my friends, but when I caught sight of him I'd prick up my ears like a rabbit and strain, hoping to hear what he was saying from a distance. My friends didn't talk about him anymore and they didn't realize that I was completely focused on him instead of them.

But Leroy no longer looked over at me in that way that excited me and made my nipples hard: his attention was focused on his new girlfriend, his smoldering eyes so deep and passionate that from time to time she blushed. I had to try hard to conceal the anger building up inside me, but I couldn't help wondering if she had ever been in Leroy's car and whether she could smell me there on the backseat. *Girl, you don't know anything about me and Leroy. He fucked me out of pure contempt in the backseat of that car. You could never be that close to him.* My heart pounded, beating with a strange sense of superiority.

Leroy's fingers, playing my body, had captured my heart. Heat flooded over my body just thinking about them. What had happened to me? Once I had been able to twist him around my little finger with a glance, and I could have had him licking my boots with just a sigh. But now *I* was fixating on every flicker of his thick eyelashes.

If this went on, I would start rotting like a discarded corpse. I had to do something. I looked at D.C. There would be no miracle with him. Hopelessness washed over me. On the other side of the room, Leroy was drinking from a glass in one hand and was absently stroking the girl's cheek with the back of the other. *She's not a keyboard. She's not your keyboard, Leroy!*

"Ruiko, are you okay?" asked a friend.

My forehead was covered in sweat.

"I'm fine. Why? Really, I'm *fine.*"

"She's much better," supplied D.C. in a serious tone. "We're back to making love every day." Everyone collapsed, laughing.

I was quiet—I didn't have the energy to get angry with his big mouth. Recently he started crying every time I tried to ignore him. It was such a hassle, I just took him to bed to avoid dealing with it.

"So, call me sometime. I'll give you my number—it's . . ."

I almost leapt out of my seat at Leroy's voice. My mind instantly became a blank sheet of paper, a pen poised, ready, and I memorized the figures as they tumbled off his lips to some woman, his familiar voice cutting through all the background noise, but far too low for D.C. or any of my friends to hear. At last I had it. Leroy's number was emblazoned in my mind, fiery, hot, and glowing.

But then I began to wonder what to do with it. Did I want more *fucking* in the back of his car? Why was I letting myself down like this now? I'd always made a point of upholding my pride in front of men.

I had the feeling something powerful was moving me along. Maybe it was some kind of divine retribution for having recognized Leroy's talent, something governed solely by emotion and totally beyond control. Why was it *so* hard, and why couldn't I break free? I felt trapped, thrashing against the sweet, sticky threads of a spider's web.

When monkeys want to get honey from an anthill they use a piece of straw. There are lots of holes in the hill where the honey is stored, and the monkey just inserts the straw into one of them, then takes it out again and licks the honey off the end. But the monkey can only get a tiny bit of honey that way, so next he crushes the end of the straw to make it look like a little broomstick and sticks that in the hole instead. That way, he can get much more honey each time. But once he takes the crushed end of the straw out of the hole, he finds it's very difficult to get it back inside again, so the clever monkey never pulls it out completely: he puts his mouth down close to the hole and keeps moving the straw up and down, licking the sweet honey from it each time he pulls it up.

How can I make a broomstick like that? I'd have to become a witch. If I had a broom like that I would stick it into Leroy and never take it out again.

But I'll never be a witch. And I don't know any magic.

Overwhelmed by frustration, I burst into tears.

"Ruiko! What's wrong?"

My friends were all staring at me in disbelief.

"Lay off, will you? I'm just drunk. I'm feeling sentimental, that's all."

They all looked at one another, worried. It was the first time any of them had ever seen me cry, and they were at a loss. D.C. was the only one smiling, the love shining in his eyes as he gently stroked my back to comfort me.

CHAPTER NINE

ix crushed, empty beer cans lay under the bed. D.C. was sleeping peacefully, snoring gently to himself—the alcohol was working nicely. I wanted to get him to sleep as quickly as I could that night, so I plied him with beer to get him drunk while he was still hungry, then filled him up with food afterward. Never once suspecting that I might have some ulterior motive, D.C. took my kindness at face value, as I knew he would, and ate and drank till he fell asleep.

I left quietly, and ran to a phone booth near the apartment. I felt as furtive as a spy on some kind of secret mission. It felt strange to be out there, catching my breath next to the phone booth when there was a perfectly good phone in my apartment, but I didn't want to leave any evidence behind—even if it was only in D.C.'s dreams.

My hand shook as I reached out to put the coins in the slot. Then I silently mouthed the numbers that had been burned into my brain as I punched them into the dial. The phone on the other end of the line, the one in Leroy's room, began to ring. I was pretty sure he wouldn't be asleep yet, but I did begin to wonder if he might be sprawled out under tangled sheets with another woman. I was mortified by what I was doing. But then he picked up the receiver.

"Leroy?"

He was silent.

"Were you asleep?"

"No, I was working on a composition."

"Do you have a piano there?"

"Yes, I'm staying at a friend's place."

I couldn't think of anything else to say.

"Ruiko, are you crying?"

"Can you tell it's me?"

"Sure I can."

"I want to see you."

"Why?"

"You know you want to see me, too. . . ."

"Shit!" he muttered, and I heard a low chuckle. "What about that other dude I saw you with?"

"He's asleep."

"You treat him like you used to treat me."

"No, I don't!"

For a moment Leroy was silent, but then he gave me the name of a hotel and a room number, and told me to meet him there. I waited for him to put the phone down before hanging up myself. Then I closed my eyes and let myself breathe again.

I went back to my apartment. There were some records scattered on the table, so I jotted the hotel room number down on one of the album sleeves. D.C.'s breathing was slow and rhythmic. But something was pulling me, dragging me away.

I had left a record playing on the turntable, and a deep, husky voice was singing the blues. I could hear the needle scratching over the grooves, leaving traces behind as the record went round and round and round.

I knew it wouldn't be long before I, too, had the same sort of scars.

I spent fifteen minutes waiting in the hotel room before Leroy finally showed up. He glanced over at me as he came in, then took his hat off and threw it down on the bed. I'd have expected him to know that leaving a hat on a bed is supposed to be bad luck.

"I'm hungry," he said. "Let's eat."

He called room service and ordered spaghetti and escargots for two, and a bottle of champagne.

"I'm not hungry," I said.

"Hey, come on, let's eat. We've never had a proper meal together."

He took off his tie and undid the top button of his shirt.

"I just don't feel like it."

"Ahh, I see. Well, maybe you'd prefer some of this instead then?"

He unzipped his trousers and took out his flaccid dick, gripping it tightly in his hand. Disgusted, I scowled up at him, but before I could say anything there was a knock at the door. It was room service. Leroy turned away and told me to let them in. I did as he said. He signed the check and gave the waiter a tip, holding his hat casually over his crotch. The natural way he pulled it off was really something.

Leroy laid the food out on the table and opened the champagne. There seemed little point in just standing there, so I sat down, too. First he ate one of the escargot, tipping his head back to slurp the spicy, melted butter from the shell. Then he wound his fork in the spaghetti, picking up a large forkful and sucking it noisily into his mouth. Finally, he wiped the dark, bloodred sauce from his lips, and taking a glass of champagne in his hand, he looked over at me. His zipper was still open and it looked as though his dick, which had been hanging limp till now, was coming to life at last.

"You're just dying to tell me that I can't hide my upbringing, aren't you?"

"Is *this* what you call a proper meal?"

He continued to eat. From time to time he would lick the tomato sauce from his lips and, without raising his head, look up at me across the table. Then, when he had finished, he leaned over and swapped his empty plate for mine, which I had hardly touched, and began eating that, too. I was incensed.

"You only asked me here to eat, didn't you?"

"Uh-huh."

As he slurped down the last string of spaghetti, he stood up. Then he grabbed my arm and pushed me down on the bed.

"Just to eat . . ."

He kissed me roughly and I tried to turn my face away, but he forced his tongue between my lips.

"I never knew you could be like this." I was seething.

"You should—you were the one who showed me what I could do. If you hadn't dumped me like that I'd probably still be happily running around after you, wiping your ass, even now."

"So you want revenge?"

"Now let's get this straight." His face took on a cruel expression as he continued. "Your dumping me was just the beginning. I really don't care about that anymore. In a way, I should be thankful. I used to play the piano because I wanted to, just because I enjoyed it. The surprising thing for me was that other people wanted to hear me play, too. And now people admire me. They treat me like a god."

"Don't talk shit. You're just trying to get me back for what I did to you. You've been planning this for the past two years, haven't you? I bet you've thought of nothing else since then. Tell me I'm wrong! You can't, can you?"

"Baby . . ." His brow knitted and he smiled. "People say I'm a genius. . . ."

I was lost for words. And my last shreds of hope disappeared, too. It was clear to me now that nothing he had done had been for me.

"Then why do you want me?"

Leroy didn't answer. He just tore my clothes off and went at my skin the same way he had the spaghetti. Then without asking, he pinned down my arms and forced himself on me. My legs were free but might as well have been bound by cord—I couldn't move.

I opened my eyes and stared at him and he stopped his violent thrusting.

"I love your hands," I said.

For a moment he looked terribly sad.

"I knew . . ." I tried to go on, but the words stuck in my throat and I swallowed hard. "I knew what amazing talent you had in your fingers and . . ."

Leroy frowned.

". . . and it frightened me."

"Look, just shut up, okay?"

But I had said all I needed to say and now I could rest and give myself up to him. He started thrusting again.

Once I'd had a slave called Leroy. By ruling him, I knew I existed and I wanted to rule forever. But my slave broke the rules and he had been punished for that.

I moaned, and Leroy slapped me hard across my face. My lip split and blood poured out. He hated me now. But I knew he loved me, too. He continued thrusting, trying to humiliate and defeat me, and I let him do what he wanted. I'd pretended not to recognize his genius and now *I* was being punished. He could do as he pleased with me. He'd earned the right.

I could tell he was feeling the same way now that he had two years earlier when he had fucked me by the piano. As soon as people had begun to recognize his talent, he had started a new life as *that* pianist. I wondered what else I could possibly do for him. Perhaps the only thing I was capable of was crying to make him feel superior.

I nearly lost consciousness a number of times, and Leroy was obviously very satisfied with his work. When he had finished I couldn't speak. My hair was plastered to my forehead with sweat and he brushed it away with his fingers so he could look into my eyes.

"Now I'm going to be living for the touch of your hands," I confessed.

"But they don't belong to you."

I started to weep quietly, and Leroy stroked my hair.

"You're just too late."

"But I've changed. *You've* changed me."

"No, you mean my hatred for you has made you change."

That was how Leroy laid out his feelings for me.

CHAPTER TEN

After that Leroy often summoned me over to see him. It wasn't that he wanted to hold me—he didn't pretend that he did. I knew he would probably abuse me, but I always dropped everything and rushed to our usual hotel room, sometimes even forgetting to put on my lipstick.

Each time, the pattern was the same. I was always hungry for him and that hunger was never satisfied. The way he screwed me was humiliating. He hurt me and threw me out of his room without giving me the time to lick my wounds. He made me feel like I was nothing, but I couldn't stop myself from going, no matter how miserable I knew it would make me.

Once, on my way back to the apartment, I got a cup of coffee from a vendor, hoping to soothe my jangled nerves. A fly landed on my hand and I brushed it away, but it kept coming back to annoy me. The vendor was crowded but for some reason the fly was only interested in me, vindictive, as if it knew all the things I had done. I felt as if it were blackmailing me or something, and that was just how I felt about Leroy.

Leroy swore at me as he fucked me. He only used those words with me. He pulled my hair and dragged me around the room, sinking his teeth into my skin, leaving bruises and bite marks all over my body. I begged him to stop, but he just laughed scornfully, and when I couldn't take any more, I'd make a run for the door.

But he was too quick for me. I'd have my hand on the knob, but he'd push me down to the floor and use his agile fingers to make me cry out in ecstasy. In my hazy half-consciousness I could see the shoes of the people walking down the hallway through a gap under the door. Once in a while, people would step on my hair as they walked by. Leroy noticed but didn't care, and just kept on screwing me.

I was losing weight. I couldn't get any food down. D.C. tried his best to take care of me, but he couldn't cheer me up the way he used to.

I became weaker as my feelings for Leroy began to consume me. I knew that even if he decided to piss in my mouth, I would have been happy to swallow every last drop. I was frantic, knowing I had to do something to get myself out of this. But once Leroy's body and mine were entwined, twisted and coiled like a rope, I gave up struggling to get free and started floating instead. Afterward I would pick my panties up off the floor and put them back on again with a resigned sigh, wondering why I had even bothered putting them on in the first place.

I always wore black underwear when I went to see Leroy because I felt like I was in mourning. Or like a criminal trying to bury myself alive. I couldn't understand why I had to degrade myself like this. I just wanted his fingers to play sweet music on my body like they did on the piano keyboard; his eyes, his bad language, and his all-knowing tongue joining in as the backup band. When they did, the melody took over my senses and destroyed my reason like a drug. His fingers were made of fire, the flames licking and burning my heart until all that was left was ash. There was no longer any order to my life. I'd lost all my possessions and I'd become his prisoner. His ten fingers surrounded me like the bars of a cage and robbed me of the will to escape. I could see his fingers and they were well within my grasp, but I knew they would never be mine.

Even though I did exactly as Leroy commanded, I began to wonder how I could get his fingers all to myself again. But I also had the feeling that if I managed to do it, his fingers would disappear altogether in their grief. As long as his fingers had any life, they would hold me in their powerful grip, forcing me to face my uselessness. It was to that extent that Leroy's fingers controlled me. I felt like a bear waiting to catch a salmon in a river in the snowfields; I could tell if it was his hand or not just by biting it. The salmon's bright, red eggs lay hidden between Leroy's fingers, but however much I begged, he would never let me have them.

Once I imagined how Leroy would make love to other girls. The image was vivid in my mind; it was like watching a movie. His open-faced expression would tell her that he wanted to sleep with her, and she would give into the guileless little boy before her. He would escort her in a gentlemanly fashion to his bed. No matter how eager he was as he unlocked the door, he would take the time to set things up right. Once they were alone, the girl would pretend she wasn't interested, but she'd let him unzip her dress and then quickly give into him. But by the time she put her head on his shoulder to show him how she really felt, Leroy would no longer be paying attention—he would be staring into space and there would be a tired look in his eyes as if to say, *What, again?* and he would smile sarcastically to himself. And although he would stroke his fingers over her skin, lightly caressing her body, she would never experience the full extent of his talents.

By now the girl would be feeling good, and she would moan softly to let him know, thinking that his fingers were nothing more than tools to give her pleasure. Then, when she was finally reaching ecstasy, Leroy would whisper lie after sweet lie in a low, husky voice, all the while knowing that he could have given her so much more pleasure if he had wanted to. He would feel frustrated with himself for holding back, but he would also be relieved that he had pulled it off.

In the end the girl would believe that she had experienced the ulti-
mate in carnal pleasure, and she would be grateful to him, never knowing how much more had been possible.

I accepted everything about Leroy. If he were mine, I would even
have lapped up the last drop of his sweat. I'd been pissed off because I
lost a fingernail when I buried it in D.C.'s shoulder, but if it were Leroy,
I would have liked to smash my nails with a hammer, bury them in his
flesh, and leave them there as evidence. My hair, on the other hand, was
too transient for that—the strands tangled up in his fingers during sex
were too easily removed.

Leroy was living in an apartment he was subletting from one of his
musician friends, and when I phoned he usually answered very curtly.
Once, however, he was actually pleasant. He said he was too busy to go
out, and he invited me to come over. I was surprised by his sudden, un-
expected invitation, but he told me that it was okay because it wasn't his
place anyway—typical Leroy—and he gave me the address.

I rang the bell and heard his voice from the other side of the door.

"Come in!"

I opened the door timidly.

It was a big, sparsely furnished room with a piano at one end.
Leroy's suitcase was laid out on top of the bed, and sheet music was scattered all over the floor. Nothing else particularly caught my eye. He sat
at the piano, and without looking up said, "Wait over there."

I found an empty spot under the open window. Leroy had a pencil in
his hand and was writing on the lined music paper. He tapped the keys
intermittently with his index finger, concentrating hard, like a small
child playing a difficult tune. I leaned my elbows on the bed, and with
my chin in my hands, fixed my eyes on him.

Once in a while he stopped writing altogether and put his cheek
down against the keyboard, remaining there in perfect silence, his lips
pursed thoughtfully, obviously not quite satisfied with what he had

written. I had the urge to go over and put my arms around his neck and hold him, but then suddenly he would look up with a flash of inspiration and begin tapping the keys again, followed by furious notations.

The sun was going down and a breeze blew in through the window, gently ruffling my hair. I had been soaked with perspiration when I walked in, but now it had dried and felt like part of my skin. I stayed where I sat behind him, staring at his back. Leroy had made the mistake of forgetting that I was there.

Suddenly he struck his head on the keyboard and kept it there, motionless. He looked absolutely desperate.

"*Why . . . ?*" he whispered. "*Shit! Shit! SH-I-I-I-T!*"

He banged his head again and again against the keyboard, strange, mutant chords belching out from the piano, echoing around the room. The keyboard was wet with his tears.

I didn't know what to say. My mind was screaming, *This is your chance! This is your chance to escape! Do it! Do it now!* I knew that if I got up, went over, and put my hand on his shoulder and held his head in my arms, I would finally be able to escape the torture. All I needed to do was to say in a gentle voice, "Are you okay?" and he would fall into my arms, sobbing quietly on my chest, kissing me.

My heart was pounding so loud I could hear it, and I found it difficult to breathe. My whole body tensed and I just sat there in the background, rooted to the spot.

"*Why can't I do it? Why? Why? Why?*"

Leroy's voice echoed in my head.

The next thing I knew, Leroy was back at the piano again. The room was getting dark and the only thing I could see was the eerie, blue-white hue of the sheet music scattered on the floor. I looked closer. Every single sheet of paper overflowed with Leroy's illegible handwriting.

He played with passion now, not just tapping at the keys with his index finger as he had before, but deftly conjuring the melody, both hands weaving across the keyboard, the piano giving voice to his new composition. I had missed my only chance to get away.

CHAPTER ELEVEN

When I got back to the apartment, D.C. was lying on the bed. He jumped up when he saw me and poured me a glass of chocolate milk from the fridge.

He stood by me, watching as I changed my clothes.

"What's the matter with you?" I asked. "You're acting weird."

"Ruiko . . ." His voice was shaking. "Have you found someone else?"

"What makes you think that?"

"Things aren't the same anymore. You're always so nice to me these day. . . ."

"Does that bother you?"

I pulled my earrings out irritably and bunched my hair up at the back so he could unzip my dress. I often let him unzip me, but it was completely different from how Leroy did it.

I began to wonder if I had left any clues that he might have picked up on. We hadn't made love recently, but that was because I found it difficult to hurt D.C. right after being hurt myself by Leroy. And after being in bed with Leroy, D.C. made love too gently.

"I'm just tired, that's all."

"You have scratches on your back."

"I bumped into something, okay? It was an accident."

"Do you really think I'm that stupid?" he yelled, throwing me down on the bed. "You're always completely exhausted when you get home and all you do is sit there, staring into space with tears in your eyes. You used to be so selfish and vain—and so happy. But now look at you! You'd never have let me push you around like this before. What's got into you?!"

"Sometimes I like being pushed around—you've just never noticed it before."

D.C. began to cry, stroking my cheek with the back of his hand.

"Ruiko . . ."

He brushed one of his tears from my lip.

"I can smell him on you."

I lay still on the bed. Although he was crying, I didn't feel annoyed with him the way I had before—this time I felt sorry for him. He couldn't get what he wanted. But then, neither could I, so I understood how he felt. D.C. wanted my heart in the same way that I wanted Leroy's fingers, so I could sympathize with him because I knew how hard it was to be in love with something you just couldn't have.

I stroked his face gently, and gave up trying to deceive him. We were both in the same boat now.

"I didn't think you'd notice. I never imagined you'd be able to smell him."

"Are you going to leave me?"

I had no response to that.

"Oh god, I know you are. You'll dump me like you dumped Leroy Jones," he sobbed.

Like Leroy Jones.

I know how you feel, D.C. But what D.C. still didn't know was that it was Leroy who was the cause of all our misery, the root of all our problems, and for the first time I realized just how stupid I had been. And now we were both in pain, hurting in exactly the same way that Leroy had been hurt all that time ago.

I felt as though D.C. and I were gradually turning into the same kind of people, the kind of people I used to despise.

"Show me your hand, D.C."

He stretched out a big, innocent hand and I gently wrapped both of mine around it. His skin was shining; it looked as though it might melt and dissolve into my own. It could never make my blood churn like Leroy's hands did. Lifting it to my lips, I kissed it gently. D.C. flinched in surprise and pulled away from me.

"Let me hold it a little longer. . . ." I pleaded.

But D.C.'s hands didn't stick to me the way that Leroy's did. They just seemed to rest on my skin, gauging my temperature. I closed my eyes at the futility of it all. We were both in the same sad, leaky boat.

"I love you, Ruiko. I really love you," he whispered over and over, knowing it wouldn't make any difference.

D.C. and I lay awake, huddled together, motionless. I had never seen him so quiet before, and when my eyes finally became accustomed to the darkness, I could see his dark, worried eyes staring back at me. But he didn't hate me. He stroked his hand softly over my skin as if he were gently caressing velvet, and somehow he seemed to know that we were both suffering from the same pain.

"I could die happy like this," I told him.

D.C. just smiled.

The white bedsheets gradually turned a dark, dusty blue and before dawn, as the night air coming in through the window began to get cooler, I greedily embraced sleep, grateful at last for the opportunity to abandon conscious thought and forget everything.

The next morning I woke to find that D.C. had already made coffee and was reading the newspaper. He drew up a chair for me and poured me a cup, and throughout breakfast he said nothing about what had happened the night before. He was carefully sticking to our usual morning routine. He seemed to have decided to ignore the problem, for the moment at least.

It was the first night I had slept well in quite some time, and I had dark circles under my eyes as a result. Holding my cup in both hands, I sipped my coffee. D.C. turned his attention back to the newspaper, but I knew he was only looking at the sports pages and the music column, so I didn't bother to ask him what was new.

"Leroy Jones is doing a special concert."

I was only interested in seeing Leroy alone. "So what?"

"It says that it's a farewell concert. He's going back to the States to make a new album."

"Going back?"

I looked over at D.C., the cup gripped tightly in my hands.

"You're kidding, right? Why does he have to go back to the States?"

"Well, I suppose that when you're in as much demand as he is, it's not easy to take a long vacation like this. He probably has no reason to stay here any longer. I don't think Japanese people like jazz that much."

"*I* like it!" I said angrily.

"So you're still interested in him? I didn't think you cared about guys once you'd dumped them."

D.C.'s voice faded to a murmur in the background. Leroy was about to disappear. But he couldn't go yet! I hadn't got what I needed from him. All he had done was take, take, take from me, and he hadn't given anything in return. Bristling with fear, I desperately tried to think what I should do next.

D.C. tried to slip his hand inside my bathrobe.

"Cut it out!" I slapped at his hand in irritation.

But D.C. didn't stop. He tore off my robe, kissed me all over, then carried me back into the bedroom to make love to me. I didn't try to stop him. I just let him do what he wanted. My mind was occupied with far more pressing matters. How could I stop Leroy from leaving me? How could I keep him within reach?

CHAPTER TWELVE

showed up at Leroy's apartment uninvited. He opened the door, and when he saw it was me he had a defenseless look on his face, and was obviously angry at being caught off guard. But I looked so pale and nervous that he invited me in anyway.

The room was much messier than last time, and there was a stale odor in the air, as if he had been sleeping and just woke up. The sheet music was all gathered together in a pile now, but in its place, his dirty underwear and crumpled shirts lay strewn around the room. In the ashtray was a mountain of cigarette butts, and on the bed the blankets were piled high like the whipped-cream topping on a dessert. A tangled mess of bedsheets was screwed up suspiciously and thrown over them.

Leroy handed me a glass of white wine. I suppose I must have looked quite ill, but the cool aroma of the wine seemed to neutralize the stuffiness in the air. He sat on the piano stool, wearing nothing but a navy blue bathrobe, and looked me over as he thoughtfully stroked the stubble on his chin. It was obvious that he hadn't taken a shower that morning, and I was flustered by his unkempt appearance; I imagined a film of dried sweat covering his body.

Neither of us spoke. Leroy went over to the record player and chose a record to play. It was only when he had turned his back that I was able to find my voice again.

"You're going back to the States?"

Bud Powell started playing, but Leroy said nothing.

"I hear you're going back to the States," I repeated.

"You gonna miss me?"

I slapped him hard across the face instead of saying, *Yes, I am.* Leroy grinned. But it was more of a smirk than a smile. *You fucker!*

I flew at him in a fury, my arms flailing, but he dodged me nimbly and I ended up in a heap on the floor, lying on my back. I looked up at him. His foot was resting on my stomach and he was looking down at me.

"You just don't understand, do you?" he sneered coldly, the heel of his bare foot pressed hard into my stomach.

His foot was big, cold, and heavy. It was like being tortured with a brick, and I was scared of what he might do if I struggled so I kept very still.

Leroy pulled my skirt up with his foot and pushed his toes inside my flimsy panties. His big toe buried itself into my soft pussy lips and I moaned loudly. Then, pushing harder, it sank deep inside me.

"I'll light your fire, all right," he said viciously, "just like you told me to in the park that night."

Christ, I hated him.

Then, removing his foot from my underwear, he brought it up to my face and thrust his big toe forcefully into my mouth. It was warm and wet, and tasting myself on his toe, I felt a sense of betrayal, almost as though I'd been forced to reveal a precious secret.

"You must feel pretty frustrated that you can't get the same kind of satisfaction from your mouth that you can from your pussy."

Oh, but I could. And my satisfaction came from being able to say, *"No."* Venomously, I bit his toe, but Leroy just pulled his foot away and kicked me in the face, then stood on my neck to stop me from moving. I couldn't breathe and I began to feel faint. I thought he was going to kill me, but I didn't struggle. I just lay there with my eyes closed.

Suddenly, he grabbed me roughly and dragged me up off the floor, pulling my hair so that my head snapped back. He kissed me forcefully, and with his mouth planted on mine, he ripped off my blouse. He sucked so hard on my mouth that I thought he'd turn me inside out. Then, removing the rest of my clothes, he bound my hands together with his tie, and pulling my legs apart, he tied them to opposite corners of the bed. It wasn't really necessary—I would never have resisted him.

Finally, when there was no way for me to escape, Leroy calmed down. He took off his bathrobe and sat down on the bed next to me with his legs stretched out in front of him.

It was a blistering summer afternoon. The air was completely still, hot and stagnant. On the floor was a sweet pool of Leroy's sweat, and his body, shimmering in the light, reminded me of a golden sunflower. He put the wine bottle to his lips and took a deep drink of the cool, clear liquid. Then he quietly turned to me and spat a large mouthful onto my face, spraying the bedsheets, the white fog suddenly turning to gold, falling gently like cool rain on my skin. I gazed at Leroy through the droplet prisms on my eyelashes, a delicate rainbow cast around his body like a halo.

Leroy began licking the thin film of wine from my stomach, his rough tongue sliding smoothly over my soft skin. The pleasure he was allowing me was not like him at all. A wind chime whispered gently at the window, the cool notes like flowing water. Without warning, Leroy sunk his teeth into my flesh. It was a delicious feeling, as though my body were dripping onto the floor like molten wax.

"Don't leave me, Leroy. I never want to stop feeling like this."

Leroy said nothing. He just tickled me with his tongue, running it lightly over my skin. How I wished that his tongue could understand my feelings. The downy hair on my body was stuck to my skin with his saliva, each hair licked clean and facing the same direction.

"I'm yours," I said with tears in my eyes.

"I don't need you," he replied. "I don't need anyone."

I gazed adoringly at his tiny nipples in the curly hair on his chest, and his stomach muscles, as hard and smooth as rocks. I wanted to kiss him all over. But even though he was within reach, I knew I could never make him mine.

Leroy buried his face between my legs and began to work his magic. I succumbed willingly to his tongue, breathing shallowly in anticipation, eager to feel the waves of passion washing over me as they grew in intensity. But that didn't happen.

"What I once accepted as happiness is now just the object of my hatred," he said, thrusting his dick into my mouth to show his contempt for me. I choked, gagging on his length, struggling to breathe.

"Listen to me!" he barked. "Suck me—slowly and gently."

I did as he said. I wanted him so badly, I didn't care how much pain I had to endure. But he pulled his body away again.

"Leroy, I want you! Fuck me!" I screamed.

He laughed sarcastically and started running his fingers over my body.

"Please, Leroy. *Please!*" I begged hysterically.

I followed the movement of his fingers with my eyes as they traced patterns over my body, but when I began to writhe and moan with pleasure, he stopped and jammed his dick back into my mouth, repeating the same pattern over and over again. Eventually I was exhausted, and although I couldn't stop wanting him, I knew he didn't want me—he was just toying with me. His fingers told me in no uncertain terms that he had already left.

"Fuck me, you bastard!" I screamed.

"You dirty bitch . . ." Leroy's fingers stopped moving.

He gave me a look of utter contempt. I was crying now, desperate for his touch.

"So you want me to fuck you, do you?"

I looked up at Leroy, tears in my eyes, and nodded. He spit in my face.

"Why don't you just kill me?"

"No," he said quietly, "I can do better than that. I'll leave you instead and you'll miss me so much that you'll grow to hate me. All you'll have left is your memories of me and booze."

His eyes were so cold.

"Leroy, don't leave me! I want you! You're the only one I've *ever* wanted!"

Somehow I thought that he would continue making love to me, even if it was only out of sympathy. But he just turned from me and said, "Looking at you now, I can see what I must have been like two years ago."

Silence. I stared at him, stunned. I wasn't crying anymore. I could see that he no longer despised me. There was no hatred left in his eyes.

He started to untie my hands, his big, thick fingers carefully undoing the knots, but my struggles had made them tighter. I watched transfixed as his fingers continued to work. Eventually he managed to pull apart the knots and free my hands.

"I love you, Leroy."

For the first time in my life I meant it. I was absolutely exhausted and my wrists burned, hot and painful. Leroy looked down at me on the bed with a sad but serene expression in his eyes.

"And I once loved you, too."

It was just an accident. Leroy lifted me up and my hand brushed against a bronze statuette by the side of the bed. My fingers clenched it and I brought it crashing down on his head in a sweeping arc. He dropped without a sound. It was only a knickknack—I could hardly believe that such an insignificant lump of metal was enough to kill him. He lay motionless on the floor in front of me. There was surprisingly little blood.

"Leroy . . . ?" I whispered.

But there was no reply.

CHAPTER THIRTEEN

P eople treated the accident like a big deal. I suppose one of the reasons must have been that Leroy was a famous jazz pianist, but at the same time, everyone wondered why such a talented guy would try to rape a nobody like me. In the end they decided he must have been crazy.

My sentence was light. The large, purple bruises around my wrists and ankles where I had been tied up painted a vivid picture of rape. The police questioned me about the deep cuts on his hands. They said they looked like someone had tried to sever his fingers with a knife, but I said very little about it. Their opinion was that my actions were simply self-defense, and I nodded in agreement.

I guess you could say that it *was* self-defense. But I was protecting my sanity rather than my body. In the end, that's exactly what I did.

When I got home, D.C. was blazing, furious about what Leroy had done to me, and angry with me for going to see him in the first place.

I was so tired I slept for days. When I finally woke up again I managed to have some of the soup D.C. made for me. He fed me himself, holding the spoon up the way he might feed a tiny bird, smiling at me every time I managed to get some down. It was a great relief to me to know that the hand holding that spoon had just ordinary fingers with no special power to work miracles. I even found myself laughing at D.C.'s jokes.

Now I can smile again, but I can clearly remember that scene under the window at the end of spring. While I still love to laugh and enjoy myself, deep in my heart I know that I am just one of those dying flowers left under the azalea bushes after all the nectar has been sucked out of them.

JESSE

CHAPTER ONE

She ain't pretty. She's okay, I guess, but she ain't pretty at all."

That was Jesse's first impression of Coco. And to her, he looked like a little fiend. Just eleven years old, but over the coming months he would prove to be the cause of constant grief and pain.

Coco was looking at Jesse's face as he jabbed repeatedly at his scrambled eggs with a fork, and already there was an uneasy feeling somewhere at the back of her mind.

Rick, on the other hand, was in a good mood. He had been happily swigging gin since early morning. But the very sight of the gin bottle made Coco feel sick after their heavy session the night before, so she was drinking iced water from a large pitcher instead.

"Ah, come on, look at her face. You can't tell me she ain't cute. I just can't stop kissing her. And she's so damn sexy, I can't keep my hands off of her," said Rick to his son, then kissing Coco again.

The smell of the alcohol on his breath made her feel sick and she barely managed to keep herself from retching.

Jesse looked at his father contemptuously and threw his fork down on his plate. He hadn't touched his vegetables at all. He stood up from the table, and turned to Coco.

"I don't eat vegetables for breakfast, okay? You got it?"

Coco was too stunned to reply. Jesse picked up his jacket and headed for the door.

"Hey, Dad. Don't worry about me—I'll get lunch at Alex's place, okay? You just have fun."

The door slammed shut behind him, and Coco was left alone with Rick in the kitchen. She was relieved that Jesse had gone. She looked over at Rick, sitting at the table. He suddenly looked down shyly, downed his gin, then stood up and went into the next room. Feeling sexy, Coco went into the bedroom and got undressed, then slipped under the sheets wearing nothing but a tiny pair of panties, and waited for him. She knew that he wouldn't be far behind, that he would follow her into the bedroom and want to continue where they had left off the night before.

This was the moment Coco enjoyed most after spending the night with a man for the first time: when you sober up the next morning and you're over the initial excitement. It's only then that you start weighing up whether you can actually get along with each other or not. And it is only when you are released from the extraordinary power of sexual curiosity that you can begin to properly appreciate each other's body.

Coco looked herself over in the mirror. She brushed her hair back from her face with satisfaction. Yesterday's makeup was almost completely gone, but she knew she was at the age when she looked most attractive without it. She buried her face in the pillow, and some of the lipstick smeared on it from the night before came off on her cheek.

She posed herself seductively on the bed and waited for Rick, but Rick didn't appear, and after a while she started to get a cramp in her leg because of the unnatural position she was in. Eventually she got tired of waiting, and crept out of bed and peered around the door, only to find Rick standing in front of the washing machine, a glass of gin in his hand, watching his clothes spin round and round in the drum.

Coco let her breath out in exasperation. She considered herself to be an expert when it came to men, but there was no chapter in her version of the Sex Bible titled "Guys Who Wash Their Clothes After Sex." The way it was supposed to be was that the first time she spent the night with a man, they would wake up the next morning, get some breakfast, and then he'd drag her back to bed again, staring deeply into her eyes as they made love, gently whispering his undying devotion and corny phrases about how they were made for each other.

"Is anything wrong?" she asked.

Rick dropped his glass with a startled yelp and turned around to face her.

"Did I surprise you?"

"A little . . ." he said hesitantly.

"Do you enjoy doing the laundry?" she asked, as she stooped to pick up the pieces of broken glass from the floor.

"Sure, a-a-a little . . ."

Rick was stuck for words, and for some reason, he reached in the washing machine, pulled out his wet shirts, and started wringing them out by hand.

Maybe he's embarrassed, she thought to herself. How old had he said he was? With an eleven-year-old kid, he must surely be in his late thirties at least. So what could be wrong with him? It was too late to start being embarrassed after they'd already slept together.

"Come on," she said, taking his hand and nodding toward the bedroom door. She led him into the bedroom and slipped under the covers. Rick closed the window blinds and started taking off his clothes.

His hands were cold from the wet shirts, and as he began to caress the back of her neck, she could still smell the soap on them. Rick had been out of bed for a while so his body was colder than hers, but as he began to warm up, he gradually started to conform to her Sex Bible rules.

Rick and Coco had met each other for the first time the night before. While their friends had been partying wildly in the club, the two of them had spent most of the evening talking quietly together and exchanging intense looks.

Rick paid her lots of compliments, but that was nothing new to Coco—she was used to guys coming on to her. When he left her at the bar to go to the toilet, he kept turning back as if worried that someone else might move in on her in his absence, and that was what attracted her to him. When he got back moments later—he had obviously rushed—he looked so pleased to find she was still there waiting for him.

Drinking seemed to ease Rick's nerves. Coco, on the other hand, was quite at home with this kind of situation; it was such a normal part of her everyday life that she even began to let her mind wander a little, wondering what sort of tired line he would come up with to try to get her back to his place when it was time to go home. But it was more out of curiosity than any sense of excitement. She was just taking it easy, savoring the start of yet another new love affair.

Rick drank like it was going out of fashion, and Coco found herself keeping pace with him. She used the opportunity to find out more about him so she could decide whether or not she was going to spend the night with him. While teasing and joking, she skillfully slipped in all sorts of personal questions.

Coco soon discovered that Rick wasn't married. Well, that was a good thing, because she had no desire to sleep with married men. Not because she didn't want to be a home wrecker: Coco just wasn't interested in other women's castoffs. Married men were so unimaginative in bed. There was no passion. It was always just sex by the numbers. Nothing made her skin crawl like a married man telling her he "couldn't live without her."

Rick could tell that Coco liked him and it was obvious that he was thrilled to have such a beautiful woman all to himself. And that made Coco feel good, too.

As they talked, he tickled her now and then, and she squealed excitedly like a little girl.

"If you come back to my place," he told her, "I'll tickle you from head to toe—with my tongue."

That gave her some idea of the kind of lover he might be, and at that point she decided she would probably spend the night with him.

Then, when he tried telling her he was younger than he really was, she could tell it was a lie, and it put her off. It was the sort of thing she would expect from a woman, not a man, so she changed her mind. She didn't want to waste her time. Experience had taught her that there was no point in starting an affair if it wasn't going to be good.

"Let's get out of here and go to my place," he finally said, as if the matter had already been settled.

"Maybe next time," she replied flatly.

His face fell and he looked down at the floor, dejected. Coco could see that he was crushed, and she felt bad. She tried to console him by telling him that she didn't sleep with anyone on the first date.

Yeah, right, she thought to herself.

But Rick fell for it.

He seemed to resign himself to the fact that he wouldn't be taking her home, and dropped the topic of sex and started talking about his son, Jesse, instead.

With his head to one side and an almost embarrassed look on his face, Rick told her how Jesse was the most handsome boy in the world, and that they were more like friends than father and son.

That piqued Coco's interest. She didn't know any kids. Her knowledge of men was almost complete, but she knew nothing at all about young boys. She wanted to see Jesse so much that she suddenly decided it would probably be worth sleeping with Rick just to get the chance.

When she stood up, saying, "Okay, let's go to your place," Rick couldn't believe his luck. After a moment of surprised silence, he leapt up out of his seat and hugged her.

"Thank you," he blurted. He had no idea why she had changed her mind.

As soon as Coco walked through the door of his apartment, she told Rick she would like to meet Jesse. He was delighted. He opened Jesse's bedroom door noiselessly and beckoned her silently.

"Isn't he a good-looking boy?"

She didn't know what to say. He had Asian features, and looked like a monkey to her.

"Yeah, mmm . . ." she replied, disappointed. She couldn't tell Rick what she was really thinking, and of course she didn't mention the part about the monkey.

She could tell that Rick was plastered just by the way he poured her drink. She watched him absently, deeply disappointed with the boy.

Sex with Rick turned out to be anything but disappointing, however, and she soon forgot all about Jesse sleeping in the next room and gave herself to the moment.

CHAPTER TWO

Rick spoiled Coco. He treated her like she was a little girl and she loved it. She was tired of the kind of love-hate relationships she'd always had with men when the relationship was equal.

Whenever they went out somewhere, there was never a moment when Rick wasn't touching some part of her. And when she was falling asleep, he would keep tapping her cheek to keep her awake.

Everything was very simple with Rick—nothing was hidden. There were no sycophantic sweet nothings or psychological games, and Coco found that refreshing. Although she felt awkward at first, she soon found that with Rick there was no point in trying to preserve the love-struck pretense she usually used with other men. It was the first time she had ever felt good enough just to relax and be herself with a man.

After a while, she began to stay with Rick and Jesse on weekends, and it was not long before she came to hate Mondays because it meant she had to go back to her own place. Every Monday morning she would kick off Rick's tired, worn-out bedcover and scream at the top of her voice, "I hate this bedcover and I hate leaving here." And Rick would rub her back gently, like he would a little baby, to comfort her. Then she would calm down a little, lie back using his arm as a pillow, and fall asleep with a smile on her face.

Coco's relationship with Rick was stable and comfortable, but when it came to Jesse there was never any shortage of surprises.

One morning Coco was in the kitchen making breakfast and Jesse told her he wanted raw eggs.

"Raw eggs? What are you, Rocky the boxer or something?"

Without a word, Jesse broke an egg into a bowl, drowned it in soy sauce, then threw rice in on top and started to mix it all together. Coco just stood and stared at the disgusting sight of him guzzling the whole bowlful with a spoon, the sticky mess turning his mouth yellow.

When Rick came in, Coco pointed wordlessly at Jesse.

Rick ignored her, instead turning gleefully to his son.

"Hey! Raw eggs and rice, right? Outstanding! Make some for me, too, will ya?"

Coco gave an involuntary shiver of revulsion as she watched them greedily slurping down their breakfast together.

"Baby, don't you want some? Aren't you hungry?"

"Are you kidding?"

"Jesse's mama used to make this for us all the time. She's Japanese, too, you know."

Coco didn't believe in God, but at that moment she couldn't help crossing herself and praying for help.

She had already noticed that Jesse usually didn't bother to use a knife and fork. It seemed that his mother had never really bothered to teach him about things like table manners. So when Coco saw Jesse grab a piece of meat with both hands one day, stuffing it into his mouth like a dog, she immediately ran into the kitchen to find him something to eat with. She searched the cupboards, but all she found was a single clean plate and fork. This house was simply not equipped for normal, everyday life.

Coco had always been taken to the best restaurants and she was used to spending time with well-mannered, sophisticated people. So eating with Jesse was a real headache. She could only hope that she never had to go out to eat with him.

"You've got to do something!" she screamed at Rick. "You can't let him keep eating like that!"

Rick didn't seem to mind it at all.

"Don't sweat it, baby," he said soothingly. "He can learn about things like table manners when he gets himself a woman."

"Why doesn't he ever stay with his mother?" she asked.

"He did at first, but after a month he couldn't take it anymore, so he packed his stuff up, got on his bike, and came to live here. He told me every day was just fighting and arguments and that there was no fun at all. If I learned anything at all from being married, it's that a bitching, whining woman is the most difficult thing in the world for a guy to deal with. And Jesse's a guy, too."

"But his manners are awful!"

"And whenever he wants to see his mama," Rick continued, "he can go on his own: she lives right near here. But anyway, you don't have to worry about it. Parents have to raise their kids and teach them manners. That's not your responsibility. You're just here because you're my girl, right?"

He kissed her in an attempt to bring an end to the conversation, but Coco's mind was on Jesse and his part in their relationship.

All Coco had ever known was the simplicity of sex between a man and a woman. Nothing else had mattered to her before. But now, for the first time, she began to realize that there might be another type of relationship: far more difficult to understand, infinitely more complicated, and completely unavoidable.

CHAPTER THREE

Coco didn't understand her feelings toward Rick. Looking at it objectively, Rick certainly wasn't the sort of guy she would normally fall for. He drank so much that she was sure he was well on the way to terminal alcoholism, and would go numb from head to foot. He never seemed to savor the taste; it was more like a race, like he was trying to get drunk as fast as possible. And he made sure he never wasted a drop—he even sucked the whiskey off the ice cubes in the bottom of the glass.

Coco enjoyed drinking, too. But Rick drank so much that it hurt just to watch him. Because he was so used to consuming large amounts of alcohol, it was extremely rare for him actually to get drunk. Coco was sure it would take at least a couple of bottles of Bacardi to do the job.

That was Rick in a nutshell: he was a middle-aged drunk with a kid. And that made it all the more difficult for Coco to understand why she wanted to spend so much time with him and why she would go crazy every Monday morning when it was time for her to leave and go to work.

The sex was great, of course. Rick never failed to satisfy Coco in bed. But she didn't think that was the reason she stayed with him. She enjoyed sex, of course, but she could say with absolute certainty that she had never been a slave to it. To Coco, it was just a pleasure shared between a man and a woman.

Rick could not be described as cool. Nor did he ooze sex appeal. When they went to bed at night, Rick was always clinging to her, his arms and legs entwined with hers. At first Coco found it claustrophobic and irritating, but after a while she found she couldn't sleep without it. He was like a warm blanket covering her when she woke in the morning, and, like a kid with a comfort blanket, she had to have him with her.

One night when they were drinking and talking together in the apartment, Rick told her that his biggest problem had always been women, and that whenever he saw a good-looking girl, he couldn't help turning around to look at her.

Cute, thought Coco.

Of course, whenever she saw a good-looking guy, Coco would turn to look at him, too. But then she would contrive to bump into him "by accident," get close to him, and eventually get him into bed. Coco knew there was no way Rick could ever do anything like that. And then the ridiculous image of him watching his laundry in the washing machine floated back into her thoughts and made her smile. Rick made Coco laugh. And even when he had poured so much liquor down his throat that he was completely trashed, all she could do was scowl and then give him a resigned smile, the way a beleaguered but loyal daughter might treat a beloved but underachieving father.

Coco liked to think that she was the only one who could really appreciate Rick's charm. His scruffy, unshaven face when he woke up in the morning, and his pitiful, sorry expression the day after they'd had an argument. Coco thought she had never seen such a pathetic face in her life. And when *she* was feeling really down, he never had a clue. He would always come out with some inane remark about the weather or last night's ball game. These were all things that warmed her heart when she thought of him. And when she realized that Rick—just an ordinary guy whom no one else thought was special in any way—had begun to mean so much to her that she didn't want to spend another moment without him, she knew that she was beginning to fall in love.

Coco laughed. It was unbelievable that she could be in love with a sloppy drunk! And as she thought about him, that sloppy, drunken face floated into her thoughts and she found herself weeping. She was beginning to see that maybe love wasn't impulsive, that it wasn't a pounding heart or some big, momentous event.

Maybe, she thought, it means crying just because he's not there. She slapped herself on the forehead at how long it had taken her to figure that out. *So maybe that's it.* For a moment it seemed mildly irritating, but then a warm glow began to spread over her.

One weekend, when Coco went to visit him, Rick was packing a suitcase.

"Hey, honey. What are you doing?"

Rick explained that his father was dying and that he would be going back to San Francisco for about ten days. He turned his attention back to the suitcase, humming happily to himself as he packed.

"Don't you think it's kind of thoughtless to be so cheerful?"

"Huh? You've got to be kidding me. This is the guy who walked out on my mother. He just ditched her, and I haven't seen him since I was a kid. How do you expect me to feel sorry for him? Shit, I don't even know the guy. All I know about him is that he's an alcoholic."

"Sounds a lot like you . . ."

"Hmm, I guess drinking runs in our family. . . ."

A broad grin spread across Rick's face.

"Aw, poor old Dad, I'll raise a glass to him."

Having given himself the excuse, Rick stopped packing for a moment and poured himself a drink. Jesse was next to him, quietly putting toys into a bag.

"Is he going, too?"

"Yeah, baby, sure he is."

"What about school?"

"Hey, I know he's got to go to school, but who's going to look after him? I told his mama that I had to go away, but she just went nuts on me. Said she wouldn't look after him unless I gave her two hundred bucks. Shit, it's not like I can't afford it—a couple of hundred bucks ain't nothing—but I'm fucked if I'll pay the bitch to look after her own kid. I'd rather take him with me and let him miss school for ten days."

Jesse said nothing. He just listened. Coco wanted to say, *Let me take care of him,* but she kept her mouth shut. She knew there was no way she could get along with Jesse on her own. He'd surely refuse to rely on her for anything. Coco thought Jesse was like a puppy—she knew he wouldn't let anyone but Rick get close to him.

But two hundred dollars? That was ridiculous! How could anyone ask for that sort of money just to look after a kid for ten days? Maybe the woman had forgotten that Jesse was her own child? But however you cut it, the fact remained that she was happy to ditch her own son for the want of a lousy couple of hundred dollars. What sort of a woman was she? Who the hell did she think she was?

Coco herself was basically scared of kids. She had no desire to have any of her own, and with a body like hers, with men falling at her feet, she couldn't imagine giving that all up to be pregnant. But while she had no interest in becoming a mother herself, she couldn't understand anyone having a child and then abandoning all responsibility toward it. The more she thought about Jesse's mother, the angrier she became.

"I'll look after him," she blurted out.

There was a brief silence. Speechless, both Rick and Jesse stopped what they were doing to look at her.

"Are you sure?"

Rick looked like he couldn't believe what he was hearing.

Jesse stared, too, a hard, piercing stare that made Coco flinch.

"Y-y-yeah, s-sure I'm sure," she stammered.

Now there was no going back. Before she could regret her offer, Rick had her in his arms.

"Baby, you're amazing. What would I do without you? Damn, I've got good taste in women!"

He was clearly delighted.

"Now, Jesse, you see you behave yourself for Coco, you hear? And if she brings any guys home with her, you just let me know, okay?"

Suddenly Rick's face changed.

"You know, thinking about my daddy like this, it makes me feel real sad. He was just a drunken bum, but he was a good dad."

A few moments later, Rick's sadness had turned to grief and he began to mourn his father, ignoring the fact that he wasn't dead yet.

Coco expected Jesse to refuse to stay with her.

"So, will you be okay with me staying here?" she asked him.

"Sure," he replied, "but it ain't gonna be easy for you."

It was times like this when Coco found it hard to like Jesse. She loved men—all men—and she thought that maybe someday she might even care about Jesse, too. But sometimes she found it hard to convince herself.

Rick was leaving on a flight to San Francisco the next morning, but instead of finishing his packing, he started drinking. Coco was beginning to feel nervous about being left alone with Jesse, so she started drinking, too. It would be ten days until she saw Rick again, and already she was hurting.

"I wonder if I'll be able to sleep at night?"

"Once Jesse goes to bed it will be nice and quiet. You'll be fine."

"That's not what I'm talking about. What I mean is, will I be able to sleep if you're not here with me?"

Rick took her in his arms and held her tight.

His face looked suddenly serious, and he asked, "Will everything be okay at work?"

"Sure, that's no problem. It's only during the day, anyway."

She sighed and gave him a weary smile.

"So how did I end up falling in love with a guy like you, huh? I had dozens of guys hanging around me, opening doors and following me around. . . ."

"Oh, my poor old daddy!" wailed Rick playfully. She knew he was trying to change the subject.

He held her close again, and Coco winced as she felt the rough stubble on his chin scraping painfully against her cheek.

When a woman falls in love with a man, she mused to herself, she'll forgive him just about anything.

CHAPTER FOUR

And so Coco and Jesse were left alone together.

Coco's friends were all very interested to see what would happen, and one by one they came to visit her to see how she was coping. Like Coco, they had never had anything to do with kids before, so they called in regularly. It was like taking a trip to the circus.

For his part, Jesse made no attempt to get along with Coco, and apart from when it was absolutely necessary, he hardly spoke to her at all. He sat in a corner of the apartment like a caged animal, listening to his music.

Coco decided that the least she could do was feed him. After her workday was over, she still had to go shopping and then cook when she got home. One day, Coco was expecting her friend Kay to drop by, so she started cooking a roast. As the wonderful smell of the beef roasting in the oven filled the apartment, Coco began to feel blue, sad that Rick wasn't there to share it with them and sad that the roast would disappear without him ever seeing it.

Coco missed Rick. When people care for each other, she thought, they want to talk to each other about their thoughts and feelings, and about the things that happen to them each day. But when there's no one there to listen, when you can't tell them those things, that's when you start to feel lonely.

Coco had only spent the weekends with Rick, but now weekends were no longer enough. Until now, she had never met a guy she wanted to spend much time with. She had no desire to share activities like brushing teeth, taking an afternoon nap, or shopping for clothes. The guys she went out with always brushed their teeth before their dates with her. And they always picked out their own clothes. Seeing Rick wandering around the apartment with a toothbrush hanging out of the corner of his mouth was an entirely new experience for Coco, and there was no difference for her between his brushing his teeth and their making love—they were both as important. So did this mean that sex and brushing your teeth were more or less the same kind of thing? Coco blushed at the thought. Since Rick had been away, she had nearly made the decision to give up her apartment and move in with him.

"Coco!"

The sound of Jesse's voice brought her out of her reverie.

"What are you making?"

"Roast beef," she replied.

"Oh, okay . . ." he mumbled.

Roast beef was Jesse's favorite. This was the first time in her life that Coco had ever considered cooking to please someone. She had begun to make something every day that Jesse would like. When Rick was there she didn't need to make any effort—as far as he was concerned, whatever Coco made was the most delicious meal he had ever eaten. Even if she served up a burned omelet, Rick would wolf it down greedily, as though it were his last meal. As only a father can, he also made sure that Jesse ate it, too. But now Coco didn't have Rick to depend on.

"I'm going out for a hamburger," Jesse announced.

She was washing vegetables, and she froze at his words.

"I need some money."

She felt as though the whole world was turning black before her. There was a long pause, but she finally managed to find her voice.

"Why?"

"I want a cheeseburger, that's why."

Coco tried to control her anger, but she couldn't stop her hands from shaking as she took a five-dollar bill from her purse.

"My mama's a great cook," said Jesse, blowing a bubble with his gum and popping it.

"What sort of thing does she make for you?" asked Coco, her voice shaking, too.

"Raw eggs and rice," came the reply.

Coco turned back toward Jesse and threw the money at him. Grinning, he bent down, picked it up from the floor, and walked out the door.

Coco opened the oven door, took the meat, and threw it angrily into the garbage can, beef juices splashing all over her and the kitchen. As she wiped her face, she wondered what the hell she had done to deserve Jesse—she couldn't believe that anyone would want to hurt her so much all of the time.

The doorbell rang. It was Kay.

"Hey, what's going on? The meat do something bad?"

Coco slumped down into a chair and put her head in her hands. She still had grease all over her fingers, and now there were bits of meat and fat all over her face and in her hair, too.

"What the hell have I done?" she wailed in despair. She suddenly realized that nobody had ever insulted her the way Jesse had, and as the anger welled up inside her, she started to cry.

"What is it? What's wrong?" asked Kay, rushing over to put her arm around Coco's shoulders.

Sobbing, Coco told her about the way she was looking after Jesse and trying to cook him something he would like, but how every night he would take great delight in upsetting her, making her feel useless and grinding her feelings into the ground.

"He's a child. What do you expect?" said Kay, wiping the table with a paper napkin to mop up some of the gravy.

A child? Fuck! Was that the way children behaved? Is that what they were really like?

Coco felt like she was going to explode. There was nothing special about cooking for someone. People did it every day. But not Coco. It wasn't in her nature to cook for someone else.

"I don't want to try to be his mother. He's Rick's kid. I'm just trying to feed the little bastard."

"But that was your choice," said Kay matter-of-factly.

Coco was dumbstruck. She couldn't say anything. Kay was right. If she wanted to live with Rick, she had to accept that Jesse was part of the deal.

"Of course, I don't know much about this shit, but aren't kids just like that anyway? Don't they do whatever they want without thinking about it first? And especially a kid like Jesse, who has never had a mother to teach him right from wrong. But you know, everybody's asking the same question, girl. Why are you sticking with this guy? I mean, he's got a kid and all. And when did you start being his maid? Come on now, tell me the truth. What are you doing? Is it curiosity? Are you just doing it to be nice or what? Guys like him with a kid in tow—can he really be all that special?"

Coco didn't know how to put her feelings for Rick into words. She had never been in love like this before and she couldn't explain it. She was confused. When it was just sex, she found that relationships with men were very easy. But when they started to become a part of everyday life, things were much too difficult. Of course there was sex in everyday life, too; the hard part was learning to deal with the toothbrush side of things.

"You're just not used to kids. That's all it is," said Kay.

She was trying desperately to lift Coco's spirits. Kay and Coco had been close for many years now, sharing their deepest secrets with each other, and now that they were adults there was little need to talk about the details. Kay just understood. Kay could sense that for whatever reason, Coco was falling deeply in love with Rick. Coco wouldn't admit it, of course. It was too embarrassing for her.

"I think I'm just feeling uptight," said Coco. "I'm sorry."

"Hey, I know you're in love with Rick, okay? But what about the kid? What are you going to do about him? If you don't think you can put up with him, you shouldn't let yourself get in too deep."

"Okay, I admit it—I don't like Jesse. For one thing, he's not mine. His mother is some woman that Rick was in love with before me. Even worse, he's living proof that Rick screwed her. But Jesse's mother has dumped him, so if I care for Rick, I've got to accept that boy, too. Right now all I want to do is make Rick happy. I love telling him jokes and making him laugh, and I love teaching him stuff he doesn't know. I love giving him a good time in bed, and, really, looking after Jesse is just another part of that—it's just something I have to do."

Kay didn't believe a word of it. She couldn't understand how a girl like Coco whose self-centered attitude was one of the things that made her so attractive, could suddenly become so obsessed with making someone else happy. It just wasn't like her.

"Aren't you the same girl that used to look down on people who fell in love like this?" asked Kay.

"All right, don't rub it in."

"I can't believe you'd put raising a child and sex on the same level. It can't be that much fun."

Coco knew that Kay was right. She felt as though she was making a very big mistake. While Coco was deep in thought, Kay got up to make her a drink, and as she did so, Jesse came home, munching on french fries.

"Hi, Jesse. How ya doin'?" she asked.

"Um, okay."

"Hey, I got you a present," she said, handing him a package.

Jesse tore off the wrapping paper and found a toy plane inside.

"I didn't hear you say thank you, Jesse," said Coco.

Jesse moved toward Kay to give her a thank-you kiss and suddenly Coco felt a rush of affection for him.

"Thank you . . ."

Kay's mouth fell open in disbelief. Coco looked at her, confused. Kay's cheek was wet. As he thanked her, Jesse had spit in her face. When she realized what had happened, Coco grabbed hold of him by the collar and tried to slap his face. Although Jesse was smaller than she was, he was a strong boy. She tried to hit him several more times without success, and finally caught him with such a hard slap that it sounded as though the bones in her wrist had broken. Jesse quit struggling. He just glared at her in silence. Blood began to trickle from his nose.

Coco couldn't quite believe what she had done. She just stood there, rubbing her sore hand ruefully, and tears began to well up in her eyes.

Any regrets she had, however, evaporated when she felt Jesse kick her—hard, in the back.

Coco collapsed on the floor, bent over in agony. She pressed her hand into the small of her back in an attempt to reduce the pain. It hurt so badly that she couldn't breathe. Jesse was insane. He wasn't human. Surely he'd been born by mistake. He was the devil incarnate.

From somewhere in the distance, Coco could hear Kay's concerned voice calling her name. She looked up and saw Jesse standing over her, the toy airplane still in his hand. His face was expressionless and the blood was no longer just trickling, but pouring down his face, a startling shade of red.

A shiver ran down Coco's spine.

"What did you do that for?" she demanded hoarsely. "Please, tell me. I don't understand."

Without an explanation from Jesse, Coco wondered how she could justify staying there any longer. Surely her love for Rick alone wasn't a good-enough excuse. Why did she have to put up with all this when all she really wanted was to be with Rick?

"Dunno."

"What the hell do you mean, you don't know? Don't you know how to thank someone? Didn't anyone ever teach you how to say thank you?"

"I *did* say thank you."

"So why did you spit at her, for Christ's sake? What the hell is wrong with you?"

"I don't know. My mama always used to do that to my dad."

For a moment there was silence. Then Coco burst into tears.

Jesse went to his room and closed the door behind him, leaving a trail of blood that led from the kitchen to his bedroom door. The conversation was over.

When Coco had slapped him, she was sure her hand hurt more than Jesse's cheek, but she had hoped it taught him a lesson. Now she realized that all she had done was hurt her hand.

"They must have really hated each other, Rick and his wife," said Kay, gently rubbing Coco's back. "How can people say all kids are born out of love?"

Coco shivered. Jesse may have been born out of love, but he had been brought up with hate. And Coco was the one who had to deal with that hatred. She wondered what Jesse was really like underneath it all. She was frightened that if she peeled off the layers of hatred one by one, like peeling an onion, she would find nothing but hatred all the way down to his bone marrow.

For now Coco was able to avoid facing that fear by crying, but she knew she would not always be able to run away. She was grateful that Kay was there to comfort her, but she knew there would come a time when she would have to face her fear alone, and the thought of it terrified her.

CHAPTER FIVE

When you are kind to people, you expect kindness in return. That was the way Coco understood the world. Hugs, kisses, compliments—there is a certain beauty in the idea of giving things away and expecting nothing in return. But at the same time, there is a distinct sadness in giving and *not* receiving. It was for that reason that Coco could not deal with Jesse. She could not show him love and affection if all she got back from him was hate.

Jesse didn't spit at people anymore, but he continued to run out for hamburgers, ignoring the fact that Coco was cooking, and he treated her like an intruder. Although, to be fair, he treated all of her friends and all of his own friends in exactly the same way. Jesse treated people like objects.

Jesse's friends were all adolescents, all on the verge of manhood, and when they were around Coco they had bashful smiles that young men get when they are around women. A couple of the braver ones would wink at or sneak a kiss from her as they came and went. They were at the age when they were naturally curious about the opposite sex, and to Coco's amusement, they were particularly curious about her.

The boys were all much taller than Coco. They left their sneakers strewn all over the hallway and she noticed how much larger their shoes were than hers. As she tidied up their sneakers she began to think about Jesse and how small he was compared with his friends. He was dwarfed by them. They grew as rapidly as if they were willing themselves to grow. Jesse, on the other hand, had no interest in getting older and seemed almost to be suppressing his growth.

Sometimes the boys would watch videos in Jesse's room. But when there was a love scene, even though it was nothing hard-core, just a part of the story, Jesse always got irritated, stood up, and walked out of the room, leaving his friends jeering behind him.

"Hey, what's wrong with you, man? This is the best part," they would holler, whistling at and cheering the girl on the screen, just as grown men did. Then Jesse would storm back into his room, screaming at them to get out.

At first, of course, they didn't take any notice of him, but when they realized he was serious, they switched the video off, cursing under their breath as they left. Heading back to the hallway, some of the kids would say they were angry with him and swore they would never hang out with him again.

They were all just ordinary boys, all looking forward to leaving home and getting away from the influence of their parents as quickly as possible. But they weren't able to do that just yet and they didn't really know what to do with all their excess energy. In a way, they were still just kids, and when they got back home their mothers would be yelling at them to do their homework. At the same time, they were old enough to have their own social network, but because of the way he treated them, Jesse was on the verge of being shut out of it.

Once, Coco looked into Jesse's room after the boys had left. He was lying facedown on the bed, thinking. He looked so vulnerable that she suddenly felt a twinge of sadness. But that sadness quickly turned to dismay as she realized it was the same vulnerability she saw in Rick when he was just sitting and smoking. Instinctively, she went in and sat down on the bed at his feet. They were unexpectedly large, and she noticed that there was a hole in one of his socks.

Coco just sat there. She felt as though she couldn't say anything until Jesse spoke. She couldn't break the silence. Minutes passed, and the silence became awkward, almost painful. She considered mentioning the hole in his sock, but when she looked up, she saw that his face was wet. He lay there silently, tears streaming down his cheeks and off the end of his nose. His tearstained face looked just the way Kay's face had looked when he had spat at her. Now it was as though he were spitting on himself.

Coco pulled off the sock without a word, and Jesse let her. He didn't move. He didn't make a sound. It was the first time she had ever touched him, and it pained her just to look at his bare foot. She couldn't believe it was the same hateful thing that had bruised her back so badly. With the sock gripped tightly in her hand, she stood up and left the room, closing the door silently behind her.

Coco went to the kitchen and took out the sewing box. She opened the lid and saw that all of the needles had been bent. *Jesse.* It couldn't have been anyone else. She sighed. But she couldn't bring herself to be angry at him for it.

CHAPTER SIX

L ife's an odd game. There are certain things that are instinctive
to all living creatures—like eating and sleeping, the things you
just can't live without. And in the case of human beings, com-
munication is an integral part of everyday life, too. Words.

As usual, Jesse treated Coco very coldly and that really irritated her.
But try as she might, she could not ignore him. He kept leaving the water running, too. At first she put up with it and said nothing, running to
the bathroom or to the kitchen to turn off the tap, but Jesse would just
go back and turn it on again. Eventually the very sound of running water began to irritate her, until she reached the point where she thought
that she would go mad if it carried on much longer. In the end, Coco
was forced to confront him.

"Stop leaving the damn faucets on, okay? When you're done with
the water, just turn it off!"

The tension between Coco and Jesse got worse and worse. She knew
that it would be far better if she just sat him down and talked to him before everything broke down completely, and she also began to realize
that she needed to employ a different tactic if she was to communicate

with him properly. So eventually, out of sheer necessity, Coco started talking to Jesse more often.

"Will you be eating at home tonight, or going out?"

"Do you want a bath tonight, or a shower?"

"How much lunch money do you need?"

"Do you need me to sign the homework you left in your room?"

Even on this basic level, Coco found it incredibly difficult to communicate with Jesse. It was especially hard because she had always found it so easy to talk with anyone. But she knew she had to keep trying.

She continued to ask him questions every day, and although he just ignored her at first, gradually he began to respond.

"I'm having butter-fried fish with broccoli this evening. I suppose you'll be going to get a hamburger as usual."

"Nah, I'm staying in tonight. There's something I want to watch on TV."

"So you're eating here tonight?"

"That's right. Hey, have you seen *Eighteen*? Mr. T's in it. It's great!"

So that night they ended up watching a third-rate drama on TV together. Although she was bored by the show, Coco sat and watched it. Every couple of minutes Jesse would burst out laughing and look over to see her reaction, the look on his face saying, *See, I told you it was great, didn't I?* And Coco had to laugh, too.

There's a knack to looking after kids, she thought to herself. But that just started her thinking about Rick because he was so easy to deal with.

Rick still wasn't back. He had already taken quite a bit of time off work to go visit his father, and Coco was certain that his extended stay meant that his father's condition must be getting worse.

From time to time, left together with Jesse in this strange atmosphere, she began to wonder if Rick had ever existed at all.

As their conversation increased beyond what was absolutely necessary, Jesse's efforts to rub her the wrong way began to taper off a bit, too.

Which is not to say they stopped altogether. For example, once when she wanted to write a letter, she found that the points of all of her pens had been broken. And another day, when she was in the toilet, Jesse was outside with a screwdriver, trying to break the lock.

By now, Coco had started to see these things more as childish pranks than as acts of malevolence, and she stopped taking them so seriously. Before she had felt that Jesse was trying to hurt her feelings, but now she comforted herself that he was just trying to irritate her. When she screamed in reaction to one of his tricks, he waited in great anticipation for her to start shouting at him. She no longer let every little jab hurt her; rather than thinking of it as psychological torture, she began to see it as little more than physical inconvenience. When it got to the stage where it was nothing more than a minor irritation, she resigned herself to simply accepting Jesse as he was.

"My mother is beautiful, you know," he said while watching TV in the living room one evening.

"Really?" Coco said, not raising her eyes from the book she was reading, all the while thinking, Uh-oh, here we go again.

"Yeah, and she keeps her house clean, too," Jesse continued. "She collects Japanese pottery with pictures on it. . . ."

"You don't say?" said Coco, feigning disinterest, but thinking bitterly, Sounds like she has no taste.

"Her house never gets messy like this," continued Jesse.

Well, that's because she never reads any books. And she's ten years older than me—so of course we're going to like different things.

"And she's a great cook, too. My mama can do anything, she's the best mother in the world."

So why does your wonderful mother refuse to take care of you then? thought Coco. And if she's such a great cook, how come all she can manage to throw together is some god-awful concoction of rice and raw eggs?

"I think my dad should go back to her."

For the first time in quite a while, Coco lost her temper.

"Just shut up!" she shouted. "If your mother is so great, why don't you get the hell out and go back to her? I love your dad and I volunteered to look after you out of the goodness of my heart. Not because I care about you, but because I love your dad. Do you even know what it is for a woman to love a man? Shit, you don't know the first thing about women, so don't start that with me. If you love your mother so much, what's keeping you here? You lived with her before, didn't you?"

Jesse glared at her. And while the echoes of her outburst were still ringing in her ears, Coco realized that he was just an eleven-year-old boy, after all. She immediately regretted everything she had said, and in her head she could hear Rick's voice telling her how, after he'd split up with his wife, Jesse had lived with his mother and she had agreed to take care of him, but after a month he had packed up all his stuff, tied it to his bike, and come to Rick's place. Jesse had told him, "Daddy, I can't live with her."

So you might expect him to hate his mother, but Jesse never had a bad word to say about her. By putting Coco down all the time, maybe he was just trying to make himself believe that his mother was better than she really was. Maybe it was just a dream he desperately wanted to see come true.

When she was calm, Coco could sympathize with him no matter how hateful he had been. But she still didn't think that, just because he was a child, it was okay for him to hurt people. She just didn't think it was right.

She didn't think she would ever have a child of her own. In fact, the very idea frightened her. What would happen if she fell in love with a guy, they had a child, and then they started hating each other? The *evidence* of their love would still remain. The child would be living proof, and the idea of looking back on lost love made her feel sick. There was nothing worse than remembering the feelings you used to have for someone you now hated.

Rick accepted Jesse one hundred percent. And Jesse still loved his mother. Coco wondered why blood ties were so strong, and how it was that sexual bonds between a man and a woman could be so weak by comparison. It seemed to her that blood ties could easily break down walls of hatred, and sometimes that they could almost make time stand still.

She was a little ashamed of herself for having told Jesse he knew nothing about women. Perhaps there was nothing more straightforward than the love between a man and a woman, and if that love was a physical love, a sexual love, two people could forgive each other anything. For that reason Coco thought that if Jesse were a grown man and she were having a sexual relationship with him, then most of these problems wouldn't even exist. Right now she needed a man. She needed a man's body. A man to console her, a man to take her in his arms and comfort her.

"Someone's at the door!"

The sound of Jesse's voice brought Coco back down to earth again and she hurried to the door. There was Greg, her old boyfriend, standing on the doorstep looking sheepish.

"How did you find me? How did you know I was here?" she asked.

"Hey," he shot back. "I'm the one with the questions. I thought we were friends, but I had to hear it from Kay that you had become a mother."

It was typical of Greg to turn up out of the blue like this when she was feeling so down.

Coco invited him in.

"I hear you're having a hard time with the kid."

"Yeah, that's right."

"Okay, just leave it to me. I'm a dad myself now."

"I didn't know you had a kid!"

"Sure, I even had to marry the mother in the end!"

Greg smiled and gave her a wink. Instantly, Coco began to feel at ease.

"Hey, man, how ya doin'?" Greg called out in greeting to Jesse.

Jesse looked apprehensively at Greg's large, muscular frame. Coco couldn't help laughing to herself as she went into the kitchen to make them some drinks. Jesse's usual tough-guy routine had suddenly vanished—he couldn't get away with it in front of someone like Greg. Greg's size belied a relaxed, laid-back manner, and he was one of the few men Coco enjoyed spending time with even after they had split up. When she came back with the drinks, the two were companionably engrossed in a TV game. Whenever Jesse swore at him, Greg just roughed up his hair and swore back. It was the first time Coco had seen Jesse this happy, and the first time she had actually seen him behaving like a normal child.

Coco smiled as she watched the two concentrating on their game. Anybody who saw them might mistake them for a close, happy family, when they really didn't know each other at all. There were no blood ties between any of them, and the only link between Greg and Coco was their feelings for each other.

Coco felt as though she had been rescued.

"Okay, I think it's time for all good children to be in bed," said Greg finally. "How about you go brush your teeth?"

Jesse didn't look too happy about it, but Greg moved over to the table and sat down with Coco.

"He's just a normal boy," he said when Jesse had gone.

"Greg, you've just met him for the first time today. That's why you think he's normal. But I'm with him every day, and he's not like this most of the time. I can't sit and play video games with him all day, can I?"

"Like I said, he's just a normal boy. He's just sulking," said Greg, savoring his glass of Crown Royal. Coco remembered how much he loved that particular whiskey, and how, when they were together, she automatically poured him a glass when he came by to see her.

"I find it really easy to fall in love with guys," she confessed. "And sex just seems to solve so many problems—after sex, a lot of the crap just disappears."

"But you don't need sex in a relationship for it to be good, do you?" he replied, glancing up at her. "Take us, for example. You still enjoy being with me, don't you?"

Coco paused for a second, then nodded.

"And since we split up, you and I haven't made love, but from time to time when I think about you I start smiling and I just can't stop."

Coco burst out laughing.

"Greg—you're still in love with me, aren't you!"

"Of course I am," he replied. "Platonic love is *such* a sad thing."

The whiskey was making Coco feel warm and relaxed.

She laughed and said, "I love you, too."

"Thanks," said Greg. "Hey, why not show the kid a bit of love, too? Love him like a brother, the same way you love me?"

It was a new way of looking at the situation. Greg had always had the ability both to surprise and delight Coco with his spin on life. It was one of his talents.

By this time she was feeling much better. She knew how lucky she was to have a good friend like Greg so close by.

They laughed and drank together till it was late, talking about their friends and their jobs. To Coco it felt as though it had been a long time since she had been this happy, and she thought how much more fun they might have if they could finish the evening by falling into bed together. But as soon as the thought entered her head she realized it was wrong, and she crossed her legs tightly, defending herself from her urge to move closer to him.

It was obvious that Greg knew Coco was interested, but he pretended he didn't notice, so they sat together all evening, just enjoying each other's company until it was time for him to leave.

At the door, as he was about to say good-bye, Greg had the same sheepish look on his face he'd had when he had arrived earlier that evening.

"Even if it has to be *platonic* love, we're still allowed to kiss each other, aren't we?" he suggested with a grin.

Coco realized that he had seen through her attempt to disguise her feelings for him, and she felt her face burning with embarrassment. She tried to think of something to say, but before she could open her mouth she felt Greg's lips pressed tightly against her own.

They kissed each other passionately, hungrily, and it was several minutes before they managed to pull themselves apart.

"I wonder if this is against the rules?" he asked her, and he chuckled to himself as he turned to leave.

Coco stood at the door and waved good-bye to Greg. She didn't feel even the slightest bit guilty. The whiskey was still spinning around in her head, making her feel dizzy and a little tired, but it was a nice feeling. She tried to be serious but a dirty smile came over her face, embarrassing her even more, and she found herself chuckling as she closed the door behind her.

Coco screamed. Jesse was standing there pointing a gun at her.

For a moment she was paralyzed with fear and couldn't say a word, but she quickly realized that the pistol was just a toy.

"What the hell do you think you're doing?" she yelled. "Don't frighten me like that, do you hear?"

Jesse stood motionless in front of her, his lips taut with rage, and he glared at her through narrow eyes, accentuating his Japanese features.

"Put the damn gun down, will you! I don't like it."

"What did you *do*?" demanded Jesse menacingly.

"What?"

"Don't pretend you don't know what I'm talking about, you bitch!"

Jesse's face was ghostly white and his hands were shaking. Coco suddenly realized what he was talking about and with a barely stifled laugh she said, "It was just a kiss."

Jesse pulled the trigger. There was a loud bang and a toy bullet shot out of the barrel of the gun and hit Coco's hand.

"All right now, that's enough. That hurt."

"I'm telling my dad," he retorted.

Uh-oh, that might be a problem, she thought, rubbing the back of her hand ruefully. Of course, she hadn't slept with Greg, but she had spent a very enjoyable evening with him. More important, though, she had invited a man into the apartment and he'd stayed late into the night. If Rick found out, she knew he wouldn't be happy about it.

"You're jealous, aren't you?" said Coco, trying to change the subject. She waited for Jesse's reaction. To her surprise, his expression changed from tight-lipped anger to pouting confusion.

"Greg's just my friend. Surely I don't need to tell you that friends kiss each other, do I? Like this . . ."

She leaned forward and kissed him on his cheek.

Jesse just stood there in stunned silence, but as soon as he saw that Coco was smiling, his face went bright red and he ran back to his room.

Coco was surprised at his reaction, but she thought it was sweet and she felt close to him for the first time since they had been living together. It wasn't a strong feeling and it was far from love, but she remembered what Greg had told her: "Love him like a brother."

And that was the moment she decided it was time to bring her stuff over to the house and move in.

CHAPTER SEVEN

O n the day Coco moved her stuff into Rick's house, she got a
call from him. She expected him to be devastated over the
loss of his father, but he sounded surprisingly cheerful.

"Hey, babe, how you holdin' up?" she asked, concerned.

"Well, we all thought Dad was breathing his last but somehow he's
made a complete recovery. He's even started complaining that he wants
some booze! So I decided to go back to my mother's place, and me and
my brothers went out to the club where we used to hang out. Then I
thought it would be a perfect opportunity to take a holiday, so I decided
to stay here for a while. How's Jesse?"

"He's fine," she replied shortly, feeling like a fool for having been so
worried about him.

Rick told her he would be back in a few days, and hung up without
the hint of an apology.

The hell with him, she thought, and began to unpack.

Coco began to wonder if Rick really loved her. When they first met
he had seemed so anxious to make sure she was happy, but there was
none of that in his phone call. While she was left at home worrying, he
was taking it easy with his family. He was oblivious to what she was go-

ing through, and although that was one of the things she loved most
about him, she was still taken aback. Anyway, he would be home again
in a few days, and then the uncomfortable situation with Jesse would be
easier to handle: when Rick came home she could go back to being a
baby and he would look after *her.*

"Your dad will be back in a few days," she told Jesse.

"Uh-huh," he replied disinterestedly, opening up one of her boxes.
He was more interested in finding out what she had brought with her
than helping her to unpack.

During the past few days, much to her surprise, Jesse had begun
opening up to Coco. When she came home after work, he sat slumped
in a chair across the room and watched her make dinner. Every now and
then something would happen—like one day, the steaks she had been
preparing disappeared. She searched frantically but couldn't find them
anywhere. Then, with an impish grin, Jesse motioned for her to follow
him to the bathroom. Sure enough, there they were, stuck to the wall
like a couple of giant red amoebas. When she turned around to yell at
him, Jesse had already run away. As tired as Coco was of his pranks, she
found herself gradually getting used to them. He was still rude to her
and he still didn't have any friends, but he finally seemed to be letting his
guard down, and his tricks seemed to be aimed more at getting her attention than causing her constant irritation.

One day, Jesse said he wanted to cook dinner. Coco agreed because
she knew that if she said no he would probably destroy the kitchen.
While he worked away, she spent almost an hour waiting nervously in
the living room. Finally Jesse called out, "It's ready!"

Coco went into the kitchen.

On the table was a plate. And on the plate there was a single potato.
Big plate, small potato. Sitting across the table from each other, they ate
it together. Coco was starving, but because the potato was smothered in

sour cream, she found it unusually satisfying, and they ate in silence as though they were savoring a rare gourmet meal.

It was through these experiences that Coco began to discover a little more about Jesse.

Greg was right—he was just a kid, after all. Coco suddenly remembered the time Jesse had kicked her and stood over her glaring with anger, but now it was as though it had never happened.

There was still friction between Jesse and Coco of course, but that was because Jesse didn't really know how to behave like a child. Subconsciously, kids play up to adults, and adults are usually happy to go along with it and give them treats like candy, toys, and kisses. But Jesse didn't know how to show the sweeter side of his nature, so he didn't reap the same rewards as normal children. In that sense, Coco felt Jesse wasn't doing his duty as a child. She felt sorry for him because she had been playing the cute card since she was a little girl, and it had never failed to work for her. When Rick came back she planned to use those same tried-and-true techniques to make sure she got her own way again. She just wished that Jesse could pick up on some of her skills and use them himself.

That afternoon, after putting away all her stuff, Jesse and Coco decided to have a snack in front of the TV, so Jesse said he would make popcorn in the frying pan. Coco loved buttered popcorn. Jesse rushed to the kitchen before his favorite program started. Coco was searching through the cupboard for things to make Ovaltine for Jesse and a martini for herself.

The telephone rang. It was Greg. Coco was already in a good mood because she had finished moving in and put all her stuff away, and now she was even happier because Greg had called. So happy, in fact, that she started chatting and completely forgot about making their drinks.

Coco had been wanting to tell Greg that her relationship with Jesse was finally getting a little better. The sound of his voice, deep and smooth like chocolate, made her smile and he told her he was glad she was doing fine. It was always nice to hear Greg's voice, so she didn't notice when Jesse asked her how much butter he should put in the pan. A few seconds later she sensed something was wrong and looked up. Jesse was standing in front of her with the hot pan of sizzling butter only inches away. She froze in fear.

Jesse leaned forward and pressed the hot metal into the side of her face.

Coco screamed and dropped the phone, instinctively covering her face with her hands and crouching on the floor. She could hear Greg shouting from the receiver on the floor. Jesse was rooted to the spot with the frying pan in his hand.

After a few painful seconds Coco suddenly came to her senses. In a panic, she lunged forward, pushed Jesse aside, and rushed to the bathroom. She looked at herself in the mirror.

"Oh my god . . ." she whispered in disbelief.

An angry red burn stretched across her cheek to her temple. It looked like a piece of cloth that had got caught on a nail and been ripped apart.

"Sorry, Coco . . ."

Jesse had come in and was standing right behind her. When she heard his voice, she exploded with rage.

"Don't you come near me!" she hissed. "I hate you! Do you hear me? I never want to see your face again. You're a monster and you can go to hell for all I care!"

Swearing and muttering under her breath as though she were possessed, Coco turned the tap on full and splashed cold water on her cheek to ease the pain.

When she finally calmed down, she remembered she had been talking to Greg on the phone. She went to the kitchen with a towel pressed to her face and found the phone hung up. On the table was a basket of untouched popcorn.

Coco wanted to cry. She tried to stifle the emotion but hot, angry tears poured down her cheeks as she took ice out of the freezer. Jesse had disappeared and she didn't care where he had gone.

She spent the night with ice pressed against the side of her face, crying from the pain. Greg called again because he was worried about her, but she was so angry she could barely put two words together. She could no longer rationalize Jesse's actions. He had scarred her face. Anywhere but her face! Her head reeled with despair.

The bond she had been working so hard to create between the two of them had snapped, and now Coco felt nothing but hatred for Jesse. He was too immature to understand the kind of love where a smile could be rewarded with another smile.

Coco loathed Jesse with a passion.

CHAPTER EIGHT

The next morning, Coco was awakened by a large hand gently rocking her shoulder. She was exhausted because she had been crying all night and the ice had melted, leaving a large wet spot on the sheets.

"Hey, baby. How you doing?"

It was Rick. She heard him put his bag under the bed. She had longed for him to come back, but now that he was here, she was too exhausted even to smile.

"Rick . . ." she said weakly.

Tears began to well up in her eyes again, and as they poured down her face, she almost forgot why she was crying.

Rick thought she was crying because she was so happy to have him back, and taking her chin in his hand, he lifted her face toward his to kiss her.

"Jesus, what happened to you?" he exclaimed. "How'd you get that? Baby, are you okay?"

Somehow Coco managed to tell him what had happened. There was no other way to explain the hideous scar on her face.

If it had been one of my fingers, I could have covered for you, Jesse, she thought.

Rick's face darkened with rage.

"Jesse!" he boomed.

At first Jesse didn't respond but after a while, he hesitantly appeared, still dressed in his pajamas.

Rick stood glaring down at him. Jesse didn't look up.

"Why did you do it?"

"Don't know."

"It was an accident, wasn't it? Tell me it was an accident."

Jesse didn't reply.

"You didn't mean it, did you? It was just a mistake, wasn't it?"

"No, it wasn't."

Coco could see Rick's blood boiling over. Unable to speak, he took off his belt, made Jesse lie facedown on the floor, and started beating him. At first Jesse endured the pain in silence, but as the beating continued, he began to cry out, louder with each successive lash. Rick took no notice of his cries and swung the belt harder still.

Coco looked on dispassionately. She felt completely unconnected to what was happening. In fact, as far as she was concerned, the blame lay squarely with Rick and his ex-wife, who had never considered the consequences of their actions. She knew it must hurt Rick to beat Jesse, but she felt that his pain was compensation for his mistakes. As he swung the belt, Coco's eyes were on Rick, not Jesse.

Keeping ice on the burn seemed to be working, and a few days later the scar on Coco's face was beginning to fade. But each time she touched it, no matter how gently, she felt that deep inside there was a deeper wound that would take much longer to heal. Now that she had time to think about it, she understood that Jesse had been jealous when she was on the phone with Greg. But surely no one had the right to feel jealous about someone he could never have a physical relationship with.

Jesse knew nothing about her. And that made her hate him all the more. Why couldn't he have simply tried to get her attention by smiling and saying, *Hey! Listen to me, too!* He wasn't a baby anymore; in another four or five years he would start going out with girls. Coco wondered if it was possible for kids who had been brought up by parents who hate each other to grow up normally. Since she had completely given up on Jesse, she just hoped that he would find himself a girlfriend and leave home as soon as possible.

A baby. That's what she was. She wondered how much difference there was between a real baby and the way she acted when she was with Rick. Jesse hadn't spoken a word to her since his beating, and that was just fine as far as Coco was concerned. She found that once she had decided to hate Jesse, she couldn't stop. Everything he did annoyed her. Even the sound of him locking the bathroom door to take a shower disgusted her. What was he thinking? Was he really stupid enough to believe that anyone in their right mind would want to see him naked? The more she hated Jesse the uglier she herself felt, but there was nothing she could do to stop it.

Rick was completely unaware of the way she felt. Coco and Jesse hadn't been getting along together when he left for San Francisco, so as far as he knew, nothing had changed. He was oblivious to the fact that they had begun to understand each other a little while he had been away.

Rick had a childlike innocence that Coco found reassuring and comforting, but that same innocence meant he was quite insensitive to the atmosphere of hatred in the apartment. Maybe that was the reason he had been able to put up with living with his ex-wife for over ten years.

Coco couldn't stand that atmosphere, but she knew it was impossible to get rid of Jesse, so to stop herself from going mad she clung to Rick more than ever. And because she was always hanging on him even when they were with other people, rumors started to spread that Rick had Coco on a leash. She wasn't particularly happy when she heard what they were saying, but what could she do? Forcing Rick to keep his attention on her was the only way she could deal with her emotions and find any peace of mind.

Rick was more than happy with the situation: he had a beautiful woman fawning over him, much younger than he was, and he wore her like a medal. He seemed just as absorbed in her as she was in him and even his coworkers were jealous. From the outside, Rick and Coco looked like the perfect couple, but in reality her mind was always full of hate. She loved him, of course, but behaving like this had never been her way of loving men.

Jesse changed, too, possibly because of the way Rick and Coco behaved toward each other. He had been very quiet since the day Rick had beaten him, but when Coco was in the kitchen Jesse made an effort to stay close to his father.

One evening, tired of reading, Coco headed to the bedroom only to find Jesse and Rick sleeping in the bed. She felt a hot flash of rage and dropped the book she had been carrying. Rick was fast asleep and didn't stir, but Jesse woke and watched her through half-open eyes, which she thought made him look sly and calculating.

"Hey, that's my place!" she hissed.

Jesse got up very slowly and went back to his room without a word. There was a dip in the mattress where he had been lying. Coco lay awake, trembling with anger and frustration. She didn't know what Jesse was up to, but the bed was warm where he had been and that irritated her all the more.

Rick woke up to find Coco beside him and pulled her close.

"Jesse was sleeping here, you know," she told him seriously, as though she were reporting a crime.

"Yeah?" he replied, disinterested.

Thinking about it, she realized it was quite normal for a boy to go to sleep next to his father. But this was Jesse. If it were any other child, maybe it wouldn't have bothered her. But Jesse was different.

Rick, who had no idea what she was thinking, pulled her closer. She tried to push him away but he was much stronger than she was and seconds later he had taken off her clothes and thrown them out of bed.

Normally Coco felt there was nothing more important than being in bed with Rick and making love, but that night she was distracted and couldn't concentrate.

The most frustrating thing was that even while they were making love, she couldn't get Jesse's face out of her mind.

CHAPTER NINE

The way Jesse tried to stick to his father was not normal. When they went out together, Coco wrapped herself around Rick's arm and Jesse always held on to the other side. Coco would glare at him behind Rick's back, and when Jesse noticed her reaction he would smile triumphantly. However much she thought about it, Jesse was not a little kid anymore, so the way he behaved was just plain weird. Rick was happy, of course, because they both made such a fuss over him. One thing was clear, though—Jesse was doing it to annoy Coco.

Jesse was very careful not to leave Coco and his father alone together, and when she caught him sitting on Rick's lap, her frayed patience finally ran out and she snapped.

"You look like a couple of homos," she exclaimed.

Rick looked amused.

"Who you callin' a homo?"

Coco pointed accusingly at them.

She was furious, but Rick just dismissed the comment as nonsense.

"Daddy, will you buy me something?" said Jesse, gazing up at Rick with his big, brown eyes. "And can we go somewhere together next week, too? Can we, huh?"

Coco just stood there. There was nothing strange about a kid trying to get his dad to pamper him, but Jesse was flirting with Rick like a woman would. She didn't know whether to pity or despise him. She felt a cold shiver running down her spine.

Coco bit her lip and left the room in defeat. Was she really jealous of Jesse? There was no doubt that Jesse had been jealous of her when she had been talking to Greg on the phone, and now it seemed that he was having his revenge. Jesse was a little devil, and it no longer mattered to her that he was just an eleven-year-old kid. He had challenged her, and now he was the enemy.

Eventually, Jesse refused to even let go of Rick. He was always touching him somewhere. The only time Coco felt Rick was hers was when she was making love to him. In a way, that gave her a sense of victory because she had a physical relationship with Rick that Jesse could never have, but at the same time she was choked with jealousy because the same blood ran through Rick's and Jesse's veins, and that was something she could never have.

Luckily, Jesse's efforts began to fail sooner than Coco had expected. He had no real experience of getting close to anyone, so when he tried it just didn't seem natural. Even Rick began to feel uncomfortable with Jesse hanging all over him all the time: he was too old to sit on his father's lap and cuddle. When Coco saw Rick push Jesse away as he tried to put his arms around his father's waist, she was jubilant. But at the same time she hated herself, disgusted by the satisfaction she derived from seeing Jesse hurt.

Jesse didn't know what to do. He just stood there with his head down. Rick wasn't even aware of what he had done. He had pushed him away without a second thought, and seeing him standing there, he tousled his hair as if to ask him what his problem was. He was totally unaware of what Jesse was thinking or feeling. Jesse looked relieved for a brief moment and turned to leave, but when he caught Coco looking at him, he turned away from her. He seemed to know that his plan was beginning to fall apart.

Once in a while Coco felt as though the whole situation wasn't serious at all, that it was actually pretty funny. And looking at Rick, sweet, oblivious Rick, it was impossible to imagine that he had a son and a girlfriend who were constantly hatching vengeful plots or underhand schemes behind his back. When she had that attitude she could finally begin to relax and feel loved again. But, later, when she was doing something like washing up the dishes in the kitchen, she would suddenly think of Jesse and her optimism would fail, crash to the floor and burn.

One day the doorbell rang. Coco opened it and found a woman standing there.

"Hi!" The woman smiled as if she assumed she was expected.

Coco was sure she didn't recognize her and struggled to find the words to reply. Apart from her friends coming to visit, it was the first time a woman had been to the house since she'd moved in.

"Mama!" cried Jesse.

Coco took another look at the woman's face. She had thin lips and narrow eyes and she reminded Coco of a drawing of a peasant woman in an old picture book she'd had as a child. She was a little nervous, but as the woman was smiling so amiably, she let her in. To be more accurate, the woman walked right in.

"Oh, my baby!" she gushed, flinging her arms around Jesse.

What can this bitch be thinking? Coco instantly remembered the story about the two hundred dollars—it was this woman's fault that Coco had been forced to take care of Jesse in the first place.

Even though she had refused to look after him, even for a few days, now his mother was hugging him and telling him how much she had missed him. Coco felt the woman was trying to flaunt her power and impress her.

Jesse looked puzzled, but gingerly put his arms around the woman's neck. Sure, they were mother and son, but even to Coco there was something not quite right about the picture.

Rick came out to see what was going on, but as soon as he saw the woman, his face lost all expression.

"Hi, Rick! You look great," she squealed.

Her high-pitched voice seemed to shake him back to life, and he offered her a chair. Then he introduced her to Coco, but his voice wasn't the same as usual.

Coco smiled weakly and said hello, and the woman flashed a huge smile back at her and hurriedly told her not to worry because she didn't love Rick any longer and she had only come because she was worried about Jesse.

Coco went to make them some drinks. All she could hear from the kitchen was the woman's squeaky voice. Rick didn't say a word.

When Coco returned to the living room with the tray of drinks, Jesse's report card was on the table and the woman was screeching.

"Why are his grades falling?" she demanded. "Tell me! I can't believe he's doing this badly just because I'm not here to look after him."

Coco felt like telling her that it wasn't just Jesse's grades that were the problem, there was a lot more besides, but this woman didn't seem to know what was going on, and Coco didn't think she had the right to know.

"You want to know why his grades are getting worse?" said Rick sarcastically. "I'll tell you why. He doesn't study, that's why!"

She glared at Rick accusingly. He refused to meet her gaze but his tight-lipped expression and narrowed eyes betrayed his anger. It was the first time Coco had seen him with such an expression.

"So why aren't you studying, Jesse?" barked the woman.

Jesse started to whimper. Coco simply could not believe what she was seeing. The little brat was playing up to his mother! Could it get any worse than this? At that moment Coco hated Jesse more than ever—more than she had believed possible. As far as she was concerned it would have been better if he had just come out with one of his usual bold, bare-faced lies: *It's okay, I'll study hard from now on, Mama!*

Rick had a sick, sarcastic smile of exasperation on his lips. Coco was frustrated by his silence, but Rick loved Jesse in his own way and he had already spent over a year looking after him alone.

Jesse continued to cry, but there were no tears in his eyes. It was just another one of his tricks, and that irritated Coco even more. Suddenly the woman turned to Coco as if she had just noticed that she was in the room and started talking to her.

"Please don't worry about any of this. You see, the problem is I hate Rick. And it annoys the hell out of me when I think that I wasted ten years on him. I know it's none of my business, but to be honest, I really can't understand why you've moved in with him."

Coco observed her calmly, taking no notice of the bile she was spouting. Her face actually wasn't that bad, but the hatred that consumed her made her look twenty years older than Coco. Damn, she was ugly. Coco couldn't bear to think that it was being with Rick that had, over time, made her so repulsive. She wore loud, unfashionable clothes that didn't suit her and made her look uglier still. In fact, Coco felt sorry for her. She was a pathetic human specimen.

Coco was amazed by the incredible effect hatred could have on a person. She shuddered when she realized that she herself was dangerously close to being consumed by the same passion.

"Damn! You're nothing but a stingy, cheating prick!" spat the woman, as she continued her tirade of Rick's shortcomings.

It took a moment for Coco to process what she had said. She looked over at Rick, shocked, but he smoked his cigarette in silence. The woman continued to rant at him, flecks of saliva flying out of her mouth. Coco found it hard to believe that a woman could treat a man she had once loved like this.

Finally, Rick spoke.

"You don't belong here," he said in a low voice. "Would you kindly leave?"

She had brought it on herself, but the woman turned pale and her lips began to tremble.

"No, I'm not leaving," she retorted. "Jesse is my son."

Jesse was looking down at the floor with his hands in his pockets. Coco was seized with the impulse to rush over and cover his ears.

"Jesse, does she look after you right?" asked the woman accusingly.

Since she was having no effect on Rick, she had now decided to switch the direction of her attack.

"No," replied Jesse.

Now it was Coco's turn to hold back her anger.

"And does she cook for you?"

"No."

"Does she ever wash your clothes?"

"No."

"Well, how about your room? Does she clean your room?"

"No."

Coco's head was reeling as she listened to Jesse trying to get at her through his mother. It seemed that he just couldn't stop the stream of lies. Coco began to wonder if he had the sign of Satan tattooed on the back of his head under his hair.

"I don't think this young woman knows how to look after Jesse," concluded the woman with an air of authority. "I think I'd better take care of him from now on."

"Coco has been doing just fine," said Rick calmly. There was no anger in his voice.

"But you heard what he said. Jesse, you want to come home with me, don't you?"

There was no reply.

"Honey, I'm living with a great guy now. You'll like him. He can be your new daddy."

Jesse remained silent. Rick held his breath, waiting for his son's reply. The choice was his.

Coco's heart was in her mouth. If Jesse agreed to leave, she would finally be free of the torturous burden she'd been struggling under for so many months.

The three adults waited anxiously for Jesse to speak. Each second seemed like an hour. Coco half expected him to try to get out of it by starting to cry again, but he finally answered.

"I think I'll stay here for now."

The tension in the room suddenly eased. *I'll stay here for now.* Even Coco had to admit that it was a stroke of genius. It was enough to please Rick, and yet at the same time it was also enough to pacify his mother.

"Oh, my poor baby. My poor, poor boy!" wailed his mother, pretending to be upset by the whole thing.

Coco looked on in amazement. This stupid bitch really didn't have a clue. She had no idea how much it upset Jesse to hear her cursing at his father. Giving birth itself wasn't anything special—the important thing was bringing a kid up and understanding him. She didn't know anything about Jesse. She didn't realize how clever or how cunning he was, or what had made him like that. She was completely ignorant. Maybe she could raise a kitten or a puppy, but she didn't know the first thing about bringing up a child. She could never be a *real* mother.

Coco didn't feel anger toward Jesse's mother anymore. And anyway, she was ugly. Coco didn't know if it had anything to do with living with Rick or not, but it certainly had nothing to do with her. She could harp all she wanted on what Rick had been like in the past, but Coco wasn't interested. She didn't want to hear it. She only cared about the Rick she knew now.

Suddenly, Coco wondered if it had all just been an excuse. The woman had claimed that she had come to see Jesse, but what if she was really still in love with Rick? This would be the only way she could think of to see him again. So *that* was it! It was all clear to her now. Rather than hating Rick, his ex actually hated *herself* because she couldn't stop loving him. She loved Rick so much that she couldn't vent all her anger on him. So even after they split up, she was left with a lot of pent-up emotion for which she had no release. What better excuse than Jesse to keep in touch with Rick? Jesse was their child, a constant reminder of their time together, and he served to feed her self-loathing. As long as she had that, Rick would always remain in her heart. Her heart was nothing more than a diary to record her grudges against Rick. But she bookmarked the pages with love.

Rick didn't return her love, so she probably hated Coco, whom he did love. The only way she could get back at Coco for taking her place in Rick's life was by accusing her of not taking good care of Jesse.

Coco considered Jesse. What on earth was he? He had been tossed back and forth by his parents' love-hate relationship, and as a result he didn't even know how to get the attention or the affection he craved. If his mother and father continued to take out their hatred on each other, there was no denying that it would eventually consume him, too.

If things continued like this, Jesse would never be able to love anyone. He seemed to know that he couldn't be happy with his mother because she was consumed by hatred for his father. But Coco couldn't believe that he would ever be happy living with *her* either. Coco didn't exactly hate Jesse, but she didn't love him either. Despite her efforts over the last few months, she still couldn't tolerate him. It was odd that she found it so easy to love Rick, but she couldn't get close enough to Jesse even to begin to touch his heartstrings. Coco felt that if she got close enough to give a tug on even one of those strings, Jesse's heart would unravel like a knitted sweater.

Jesse's mother started getting ready to leave. She looked completely different now from when she had arrived. She picked up her bag and swung it violently across her shoulder. It hadn't been properly closed, so all of the contents fell out and scattered across the floor. There was a cheap lipstick, a worn-out wallet, and a gaudy handkerchief, none of which matched her heavy makeup or her haughty attitude. She scrambled around on the floor to pick them up, and it reminded Coco of Millet's painting of French peasant women bent double in the fields collecting the broken heads of wheat after the harvest—the scraps. Coco felt sorry for her. Scraps were all she would have from now on, whomever she found to love.

Rick didn't move. He watched her but said nothing. Jesse, on the other hand, instinctively got down on his hands and knees to help. So he *was* able to express his love, thought Coco. The question was whether his mother could accept that love. She had refused to look after him unless she was paid for it. Maybe she, like Jesse, could take love but not return it.

"Take care of yourself, Jesse," she said. "Next time I'll take you with me."

Coco showed her to the door.

She said good-bye to Jesse as she left, but she didn't even go through the motions of thanking Coco or asking her to continue to look after her son for her. She just turned and left with angry eyes and a furrowed brow. That made it all the more clear to Coco that her visit had just been an excuse to see Rick and had nothing to do with Jesse at all.

As she watched her walk away, Coco felt as though all the energy had been drained from her body. She was frightened to go back into the apartment because she knew that the atmosphere of hatred she detested so much would be lingering there. The air would be thick with it, stifling and cloying, and it would be hard to get the stench out of her nostrils.

CHAPTER TEN

That night Rick went out. He didn't tell Coco where he was going and, even after it got late, he did not return. As he had been putting his jacket on, she had wanted to ask him not to go, but she knew that he couldn't bear the poisonous atmosphere in the apartment and she knew he was the type of man who ran away from situations like this.

One reason she didn't want him to leave was that she didn't want to be left on her own with Jesse. She wanted to ask the boy why he had lied about her to his mother, but without Rick she didn't have the courage to face him.

After his mother left, Jesse had gone to his room and hadn't come out. Coco sat alone in the living room with a bottle of gin in her hand, feeling very lonely. Why was it that a man and a woman could be so happy together, but when someone else got involved it could all go so horribly wrong? It wasn't as though she had hated Jesse from the beginning. She had wanted to accept him as a part of Rick's life.

Coco remembered how hard she had tried to look after Jesse. Before she met him, she had only to smile and she would be rewarded by a thousand compliments from adoring admirers. But she had thrown all that away to work like a slave, and she received nothing in return. Before, she had been happy because Rick had kept her warm and had made her feel loved; she could just close her eyes and ears and ignore everything else. But things were different now. And Rick's hugs and kisses didn't make up for what she was going through. It was a bit like eating a delicious meal in a high-class restaurant—once you had finished what was on the table, there wasn't any more. And after the initial pleasure of eating had passed, she found it was quickly replaced by much darker thoughts and feelings. Those feelings frightened her because they began to pull together, gradually solidifying and taking shape, slowly turning into Jesse.

Since he was very small, Jesse had been brought up in an atmosphere of pure hatred and he had been powerless to object. That hatred had formed layers around him, enveloping his whole body, but it wasn't *his* hatred. It was his parents' hatred for each other. Coco wondered if she could strip off those layers. Or maybe she could smash them with a single blow, crack them open like the rock-salt shell around salt-baked chicken, and suck the tasty chicken gravy from the broken lumps of salt.

Right now, Coco wanted a man. She knew it wouldn't solve her problems, but she felt she needed a taste of paradise, however brief. But Rick wasn't there for her.

The gin hadn't lit a fire in her heart yet either, and although all the things she wanted to say to Jesse were whirling around in her mind, she still was not able to spit them all out and tell him what she thought.

Coco sat alone in the living room, not knowing what to do with her emotions, when Jesse suddenly came out of his room and sat down on the sofa opposite her as though it were the most natural thing in the world. She was amazed. She didn't understand how his attitude could change so easily.

He calmly opened a magazine and began to read. Coco was thoroughly confused. The way he was behaving was so seemingly nonchalant that she could no longer understand what his true intentions were. And though she had so many things she wanted to tell him, she didn't know where to start.

"Daddy's late," said Jesse without looking up from his magazine.

He was right. Coco's concern immediately shifted to Rick. Where was he?

"If Daddy was with someone else, would you be upset?" he asked.

Someone else? Another woman? Now Coco really began to worry.

"Would you hate him if he was?"

She looked deep into his eyes, but Jesse wasn't wearing his usual know-it-all expression. He just stared back at her, the look in his eyes imploring her to say she could never hate his father.

"If he was with someone else? I've never thought about it," she replied falteringly, almost in tears.

"Hey, no point worrying about it. He was off with other women all the time when he was with my mama!"

Coco's heart began to pound. Jesse seemed sure that Rick was with another woman, but she found it difficult to believe that Rick would ever leave her at home and go off with someone else. Especially since he had always shown her so much love and affection and had seemed so sincere. She tried hard to dismiss the idea, but now that the seed of doubt was in her mind, it began to grow.

What if he really was? What would I do? she wondered.

"Whiskey and women," said Jesse, imitating Rick, "the best medicine! Ain't that right?"

Coco's eyes filled with tears, and one by one they began to fall. She was overwhelmed by all the emotions she had been trying so hard to control, and, unleashed, they took the form of a river of tears flowing down her cheeks. She felt as though she were deflating, shriveling up inside.

Jesse just stared at her in surprise.

With her head in her hands, Coco's face was covered, but through the gaps between her fingers she could see Jesse's feet. He wore dirty basketball shoes and she noticed for the first time that his feet were bigger than hers now. He shuffled closer and she felt his hand gently patting her trembling back. Then Jesse was sitting next to her, quietly stroking her back as she sobbed.

It felt so good; Coco didn't want to stop crying. Her feelings of anxiety had already dissipated but in spite of that she continued to cry. It was almost as though it was easier to keep crying than to stop. But it was too sweet a feeling to blame simply on inertia.

Jesse snatched his hand away from her back as he heard the sound of Rick's key in the lock, sending a sudden, nervous twitch through Coco's body.

Rick seemed a little surprised to see them together, but he calmly walked into the room and sat down.

"Can you get me some gin, too?" he asked.

He was drunk, but not so drunk that he couldn't talk. Coco poured him a gin and lime, turning away to hide her tear-streaked face.

Without a word, Jesse got up to go back to his room, but Rick told him to sit down again.

"Do you have something to say for yourself?"

Jesse shrugged his shoulders as if to say he didn't know what Rick was talking about.

"Don't you like Coco?" he asked.

There was no reply.

"Answer me!" he demanded.

It was one of the few times Coco had seen Rick command any respect from Jesse, and she waited to see what would happen.

"It's not that I don't like her," said Jesse hesitantly.

"Well, it certainly doesn't seem like it. Why don't you try showing it sometime? Listen, I know you love your mama and that you'd like it if we got back together, but you know that ain't gonna happen. Me and your mama have never been able to get along with each other and we always end up fighting. You know that."

Jesse nodded.

"Coco loves me," Rick continued. "And that's why she's been trying so hard to look after you, doing all the cooking and cleaning and shit. She's doing it for you, not because she enjoys it. When I feel hungry I can go out and get something to eat. And when I don't have anything to wear, I can go out and buy myself some new clothes. And if this place is dirty, it ain't gonna kill me. So why do you think she's doing it? It ain't no volunteer work. She's doing it because she loves me. And how do you pay her back? Have you ever thanked her? Even once? I'm telling you straight now, Jesse, looking after you should have been your mama's job. But she never made the effort. She never tried. Coco *is* making the effort, though. She *is* trying. Do you understand what I'm saying?"

Jesse nodded again, but as she listened to what he was saying, Coco couldn't look Rick in the face. She had told her girlfriends that she considered Jesse a volunteer project; she had even told him that to his face.

"Your problem is that you just don't like me having a girlfriend. You want me to be with your mother, don't you? Shit, I understand that. And if this were a normal family, that would be fine. But this ain't a normal family, is it? Today was a perfect example—me and your mama, we hate each other. Can you imagine how that feels? Well, let me tell you, it's the worst feeling in the world. I don't know about you, but I just want to be happy—that's all. When I married your mama, I was too young to make her happy. And when she was unhappy, that made me unhappy, too. Now all I want is to be happy."

He took a sip of his gin.

"Just think about it—when I die, you'll be the one who suffers most. I guess Coco will be sad and cry a little, too, but she'll have no problem finding someone to take my place when I'm gone. But what can you do?

You can't go out and get yourself a new daddy, can you? You've only got one daddy and that's me. So until you're big enough to fend for yourself, you're gonna need me. I am your dad. Aren't I important to you? Don't you even care if I'm lonely because I don't have someone to love? Right now I need Coco. And if she leaves because of you, how do you think that's going to make me feel? Are you gonna tell me you want me to live without a woman? That ain't fair, Jesse. I've got a woman and that woman is Coco. So if you want me to keep on being your dad, you're going to have to start accepting her. I don't think you understand how great it feels to be in love. It's great. There's nothing better."

Jesse appeared to be deep in thought. But Coco wasn't happy just to hear that Rick loved her. She knew that if Jesse decided to bite the bullet and force himself to accept her for Rick's sake, while they might be able to get along with each other, they would never have more than a super-ficial relationship. That was all she had wanted in the beginning, of course, but that didn't seem to be enough anymore, especially since she had met his mother.

"Did you used to love Mama as much as you love Coco now?" asked Jesse finally.

"Yes, I did. But I loved her in a different way. Don't you think Coco's a nice girl? You know, being in love is the best, man. Why don't you try to love her, too?"

Jesse looked down at the floor in silence. The pages of the magazine on his lap had been scrunched up in frustration.

"Don't you like her?" pressed Rick.

"It ain't like that. . . ."

"Okay, I'll tell you what I think. I think you've already started liking her. But you see, the thing is, when you like a girl, you've gotta tell her. If you don't tell her you like her, she'll run away."

"I . . . I . . . I . . ." Jesse began to whine. "I hate her!" he shouted, and burst into tears. His sobs sounded like the howls of a little wolf.

"I love my mama," he sobbed. "I love my mama!"

Coco sighed. It was over. Jesse may have been wrapped in layers of hate, but underneath it all he was full of love—unrequited love for his mother.

Now Coco knew what she had to do: she had to leave. She knew it would take time to get over Rick and that she would be very sad for a while, but as he had explained to Jesse, that pain would disappear. She would just have to get used to the idea of losing him.

There were no tears in her eyes this time. She felt as though all the time she had spent with Jesse had been leading up to this moment. What had started as a chance meeting had developed into a challenge, and at one point, she thought she was getting close to Jesse. She remembered the time she had thought Jesse was beginning to warm to her a little. Sure, he had given her a hard time, but in a way he couldn't help it. He knew what love was, but however much he tried to express his feelings, the thick layer of pain wrapped around his heart would not allow him to show it. Coco could not imagine how much the internal conflict must have hurt him. Rick had told Coco he loved her, but Jesse needed him most.

Jesse cried as if his guts were being wrenched out. Rick had never seen him in such a state before and just looked on in silence. As usual, Rick didn't understand what was going on. Someday, thought Coco, the fact that they had the same blood running through their veins might help solve their problems and make everything all right again.

Coco had made up her mind.

"Jesse," she said quietly, "I've decided it would be best for me to leave. You listen to what your daddy tells you, okay? And you might not believe me, but just remember that I really tried my best to get along with you."

The howls had subsided, but Jesse hung his head and continued to cry. Coco felt as miserable as if she had been dumped by a boyfriend.

Usually, whenever she went after a guy, he would fall madly in love with her and everything worked out fine. But this time, things hadn't gone as she had expected.

"Coco, don't leave me," whispered Rick falteringly.

She hesitated. Rick didn't look exactly lost, but she could hear a note of despair in his voice.

"Jesse, if you don't say something now, it's gonna be just the two of us again."

Coco didn't expect Jesse to say anything, but even if he did, and even if he tried to stop her from leaving, she knew it wouldn't be because he wanted her to stay, but because his father had asked him to.

Jesse stood up and opened his mouth as if he was about to speak. Coco waited to hear what he had to say. She was sure it would be the last time they spoke to each other.

"I . . . I . . ." stammered Jesse, then he groaned and lurched forward, violently throwing up his lunch all over the carpet.

Coco stood and watched, not even moving forward to rub his back. He continued to retch painfully and after a few moments she noticed blood was pouring out of his nose, too. She grabbed a box of tissues from the table and was about to wipe the blood away when the howling started again.

Blood, vomit, and bestial howling. Coco could not believe the scene that had unfolded before her. The whole thing was so upsetting that she didn't know what to do next. And then Jesse spoke.

"I love Coco," he spluttered. "If she loves me, I love her, too."

It was the sound of the rock salt cracking.

Jesse finished throwing up, rinsed his mouth out in the bathroom, and without another word, went up to bed.

Coco was in a daze, but Rick's voice brought her to her senses. He was smiling. He had just been sitting, watching them the whole time.

"Well," he said, standing up from the table, "I don't want to clean *that* up!"

He motioned toward the stinking mess all over the carpet. Coco knew it would be up to her to take care of it and the idea made her feel sick.

She knew she wouldn't be able to leave right away, and she felt as though she had somehow been tricked into staying. She decided to take her time clearing up the mess—first she had something she wanted to ask Rick.

"Who were you with tonight?"

Rick burst out laughing.

"I wasn't with anyone—I was alone," he replied.

She told him what Jesse had said.

Rick knitted his brow in feigned concentration.

"I am not . . ." he began.

Coco took a deep breath. She was sure she was going to be angry.

"I'm not that young anymore."

And with those few words, she knew she'd lost her chance to escape.

"Come to bed when you're finished," Rick told her, heading to the bathroom.

While cleaning up the filthy remains of Jesse's lunch, it seemed to Coco that that was a much better idea than leaving.

CHAPTER ELEVEN

The next morning, Coco woke up next to Rick. She looked in Jesse's room but he had already left the house, and the kitchen table was littered with bits of breakfast cereal.

She remembered making love the night before. Rick had been so gentle with her that it felt as though he was soothing away all the aches and pains she had suffered since she had moved in with him. It wasn't the same sort of aggressive, passionate sex they'd had together when they first met, but it made Coco feel relaxed, like she had spent her whole life in bed. And it had been quite a while since Coco had been in bed with Rick without being disturbed by the image of Jesse's face in her mind.

After Rick fell asleep, Coco lit herself a cigarette. It gave her a peaceful feeling to watch him sleeping. And it was that feeling, she told herself, that was the reason she was throwing her former life away for him. Of all the other men she had been with, who else had been able to make her feel like this? It was like sand in an hourglass. An upside-down hourglass. But you couldn't tell which way was the right way up anymore. The more you looked at it, the more an upside-down hourglass stopped being upside down, and like the sand, her feelings flowed silently, never ending.

Jesse came back at lunchtime and acted as if nothing had happened the night before. He ate the lunch Coco made for him and thanked her, then left again. Coco just watched, refusing to believe he could have forgotten what had happened. She could see that he was making an effort to accept her, but she couldn't understand what had made him change his mind.

Jesse had said that if Coco loved him, he would love her, too. Very cunning. In the end he'd managed to put the burden on her—she was the one who had to make the first move. It was almost funny. Coco used to look down on women who had to make an effort to be loved.

Rick was getting ready for work, checking through some papers for the night job he had started recently. He seemed aware that Coco had slept soundly in his arms the night before and acted as if he didn't have a care in the world. He believed that everything was okay as long as Coco was smiling and Jesse was safe. "Okay" was enough for Rick, and Coco wasn't irritated by that. In fact, she thought all their problems could be solved if she could only be as easygoing as he was. She was envious of him, and when she looked at him it reminded her of how weak she really was.

After Rick had gone to work, Coco finished eating dinner with Jesse in silence and later settled down to read a book. She avoided talking to Jesse and whenever he caught her eye or tried to say something, she felt awkward and looked away. To her surprise, she felt shy when Jesse looked at her. It was almost like she was a teenager in love again.

After a few days, Jesse started looking at her strangely. Now that he had stopped playing tricks on her and he wasn't annoying her anymore, she had started to avoid him. Maybe he realized she was staying out of his way, and that was why he stopped waking her in the morning to make his breakfast and started making it himself. From the bedroom,

Coco could hear him in the kitchen. She knew what he was doing, but she didn't bother getting up. It didn't occur to her to help him. Maybe she was just trying to avoid his eyes. She didn't know how Jesse saw her anymore. It was only when she heard him get his bag and close the door behind him that she could relax again. With Rick snoring beside her, exhausted from working the night shift, she was able to just go back to sleep.

One night, she woke to the sound of fire engines. It sounded like there was a fire close to their apartment, and she could hear the neighbors getting up to go out and see it. She told herself it wouldn't be a big fire and nestled back under the comforter, but the buzz of people outside the apartment prevented her from falling back to sleep. She always got scared when Rick wasn't at home and there was something happening outside. She could hear Steve next door kicking up a fuss, so it wasn't long before she was wide awake.

As she tossed and turned, there was a knock on the bedroom door. Without waiting for an answer, Jesse came in. She wondered if he was unable to sleep because he was scared by the fire, but his face was excited and he talked rapidly.

"Hey, Coco, you want to go see the fire? It must be a really big one."

"I'm not sure. . . . It's cold out there."

"We could watch it from the balcony."

Reluctantly, she got out of bed and put her dressing gown on, but she had to admit that she was curious about just how big the fire was.

Walking through the apartment with the lights off, Coco bumped into the table and stumbled over one of the chairs. She cursed under her breath, but Jesse took her by the hand and led her over to the window. He was so excited about the fire that he didn't seem to realize he was holding her hand.

Coco realized, of course, but she was too surprised to pull it away. Jesse's hand wasn't small like hers. It wasn't as soft as hers either. It had the muscles and veins of a man's hand. Nervous in case he realized her palm was already sweating, she tried to relax as they stepped out onto the balcony together.

The fire seemed farther away than she had expected, but it was a big fire and it was out of control; the sky glowed red above it. Their neighbor Steve was out on the road in front of the apartment, talking loudly about the fire and where it had broken out.

Jesse gazed out over the balcony at the raging downtown fire. Bathed in the incandescent glow, he looked so pure and innocent. Until a moment earlier, he had been holding Coco's hand, and now it felt as though that hand were the only part of her body that was warm.

There were lots of fire engines, sirens wailing and lights flashing. Coco felt cold and pulled her dressing gown tightly around her. Jesse was clad in just his pajamas, but he didn't seem to feel the cold as he stared at the fire. Coco couldn't find anything to say.

Finally, Jesse spoke.

"Are you scared?" he asked, as if he had just noticed her standing next to him.

"No, just cold," she replied.

"You can tell me the truth. I know you're scared really, aren't you? Girls are all the same. They get scared over every little thing and then they start crying."

"No, really, I'm not scared at all. The fire's way over there and will never reach us here."

"Okay, you can say what you want. I know you're really scared. But listen, you don't need to worry, okay? I'm here with you. Daddy's not here, but I am."

Coco was speechless. Jesse had seen straight through her and found her weak spot. She was a grown woman and he was still just a little kid, but their roles had been reversed—in Jesse's mind. He had decided that, as a woman, Coco was the weak one, whereas he was on the verge of manhood.

He'd realized that Coco was in a difficult position and he knew that she might have to leave the man she loved if he didn't do something to prevent it. He was beginning to understand his role as a man; that it was part of his job to protect the weak. Maybe he finally understood that when he saw Coco's reaction when he tried to look at her.

As for Coco, she was able to see that, now that he knew she could never be his mother, Jesse was trying to treat her like a lady—a lady who was living with him and his father. In that instant a great weight lifted from her shoulders, and she was finally able to tell him how she really felt.

"I don't want to be your mother," she said.

The tangled thoughts flying around inside her head had formed a single, simple sentence as the words left her mouth.

"I know," replied Jesse, "I've already got a mama. You're my dad's girlfriend."

"And I love your dad."

"I know that, too, but what I don't understand is why you like him. He's just a damn drunk."

"Of course you don't understand. You're still just a kid. You don't even have a girlfriend yet."

"Yeah? Well, maybe that's because I'm a homo . . ."

"What?"

"I'm only joking!" he said with a grin. "Oh, shoot, the fire's gone out already."

Coco could hardly believe she was finally having a normal conversation with Jesse! She was almost in tears. It was exactly what she had wished for all along. She didn't want gratitude for her efforts to look after him. And she didn't want him to love her like his mother. She just wanted him to treat her like a woman.

Coco put her hand on his back as she followed him in from the balcony. He was so skinny that she could feel his ribs and each of the bones in his spine. No love. No layers of hate. Just bones.

Jesse said good night as he went back to his room and closed the door behind him. Then he opened it again and stuck his head out.

"Hey," he said with a shy grin, "are girls really that great?"

Coco stifled a laugh. He would remember what his dad had told him till he found out the truth for himself.

"You'd better believe it," she replied with smile. "And men aren't that bad either."